What people are saying about
The Crumbling Empire

"This is a work of fiction... or is it? Compelling, true to life, and very believable, drawn from the author's personal experience and the sad and tortuous history of a long line of predatory clergy and institutionalized cover up."

-Rev. Robert M. Hoatson, Ph.D.
Co-Founder and President
Road to Recovery, Inc.

"This is a compelling thriller you will find hard to put down until you reach the final resolution. It is written with great passion, as one of the two authors was himself a victim of a predatory Roman Catholic priest as a boy. His sister and co-author witnessed first-hand the resultant suffering her brother experienced and together, the pair weaves a believable tale of suspense.

We are promised further novels about Ben, the protagonist in this story, and I look forward to their publication.

-Ian Mayo-Smith, M.B.E., Ph.D., M.A., Emeritus Professor,
Univ. of Connecticut

"A wonderful and riveting story... I look forward to a film adaptation and think it will make for a great vision on screen."

-Paul Lopes, Screenwriter

THE
CRUMBLING EMPIRE

THE
CRUMBLING EMPIRE
The Vatican on its Knees

E. Brian Walsh
and M.W. Satchell

Meriden, Conn.

To Joyce, Jimmy, Angela, David, Kris, Pete, Millie, Charlie, and our brothers and sisters who share our history and our hearts.

Preface

This is a book of fiction based on a societal ill that is very real, leaving in its wake the scarred and shattered lives of hundreds of thousands of children and adults around the globe. It is time that the parties involved are held accountable. It really is time. Read on.

"...for the first time in Ireland, a report into child sexual abuse exposes an attempt by the Holy See to frustrate an inquiry in a sovereign, democratic republic ... as little as three years ago, not three decades ago," Enda Kenny, the Taoiseach, or Prime Minister of Ireland told his government in 2011 following release of the Cloyne Report, an Irish government report that revealed coverups by the church leaders of the rural diocese of Cloyne which were encouraged by the Vatican.

The Cloyne Report, Kenny noted, "excavates the dysfunction, disconnection, elitism — the *narcissism* — that dominate the culture of the Vatican to this day."

'The rape and torture of children were downplayed or 'managed' to uphold instead, the primacy of the institution, its power, standing and 'reputation,'" he concluded.

The Prime Minister's vocal repudiation of the Vatican's behavior set off a firestorm and led to the recall of the Vatican's Papal Nuncio to Ireland. Later that year, Ireland closed the Vatican embassy, a stunning move by a country whose close ties to the Roman Catholic Church had never before waivered. Relations between the Vatican and Ireland's Prime Minister remain frosty and Ireland's practicing Catholic population is half what it was even a decade ago, according to knowlegable observers.

As extensive as the problem in Ireland is, one in five persons alive today have been sexually molested as a child around the world, either by a member of the clergy, or a family member or other perpetrator. In the U.S., some 11,000 documented allegations of sexual abuse of minors at the hands of Roman Catholic priests or deacons were reported between 1950 and 2002, according to a report commissioned by the U.S. Conference of Catholic Bishops on the subject. Produced by John Jay College of Criminal Justice, the report found that during those years, there were 6,700 substantiated accusations against 4,392 priests in the U.S. Of these documented cases, 1,021 of these were reported to the appropriate law enforcement authorities. More than 3,000 were not investigated because the perpetrator was deceased. A total of 100 prison sentences were handed down.

Young survivors of clergy sexual abuse experience unspeakable traumas that often reach far beyond the assault itself. The typical long-term consequences of sexual abuse of minors is extensive and is both physical and psychological. It is extremely detrimental to the victim in forging appropriate relationships later in life. Anxiety and feelings of failure can overtake the victim leading to a host of addictive behaviors, post-traumatic stress disorder, and even suicide. In short, the effect of the abuse is not short-lived and incident-specific, but rather, lifelong as it kills the victim's chance for an emotionally healthy future.

Acknowledgements

One in five persons alive today have been sexually molested as a child. Brian was one of them. We recognize he and countless others wouldn't be alive today without the support and insight they received from Survivor's Network of those Abused by Priests (SNAP). We extend heartfelt appreciation for SNAP's efforts, and special appreciation to Beth McCabe, Jim Hackett, Bob Hoatson, David Clohessy, Barbara Blaine, Tim Walsh and Dick Regan for their courage in the fight for the dignity of children and adults who have been forced to experience such trauma, and for their efforts in protecting these victims' most basic of human rights.

We would also like to acknowledge other organizations who have worked to address these issues, including The Global Alliance, National Survivor Advocates Coalition, One in Four, The Road to Recovery, BishopAccountability.org. And we have to acknowledge courageous individuals including Andrew Madden, Enda Kenny, Archbishop Diarmuid Martin, and many others who bravely soldier on to call attention to this scourge and hold perpetrators and the Vatican accountable. We realize there are many, many other groups and individuals out there involved in this issue, and we extend our thanks and gratitude to all of you.

Contents

PART ONE

Fumata Nera

page 1

PART TWO

The Unfolding

page 47

PART THREE

Retribution

page 85

PART FOUR

Power Play

page 155

PART FIVE

The Settlement

Page 211

PART ONE

Fumata Nera

Chapter 1
Fumata Nera

Black smoke billowed from the Sistine Chapel. Below, tens of thousands of Roman Catholics and news crews from around the globe held their breath in St. Peter's Square. After the aging Pope's death four weeks earlier, a new Pope was finally being elected.

An ocean away, Ben Clancy awoke in the mid-afternoon from a brief nap with hair askew. At age 57, Ben kept his life simple, workable, orderly. Used to living alone, he turned on the coffee, did a set of pushups and took a cold shower to clear his head.

Freshened up and ready for the rest of the day, Ben switched on the television, more for background noise than to pay attention, as he checked his email. The wiry, still attractive, salt-and-pepper-haired Ben looked up briefly and listened as the news from Rome was announced on CNN. He then returned his attention to his email inbox. Though he was raised Catholic, Ben had lost his faith in the Church ages ago. A Buddhist altar on a center wall in his study showed the level of commitment he had toward Eastern philosophy, something he had actively pursued for many years. Ben found it deeper, richer and more honest than dogma-laced Western Religions. Plus he enjoyed his own personal growth by applying its many lessons. In short, he found it liberating.

Ben went to his apartment complex mailboxes and collected his daily mail. There was little there except for a bill, which by habit, he paid promptly. He lived a life that was orderly, precise, and diligent and the check was in the mail a short while later. No surprise to those who knew Ben as a child and upon entering high school, but it wasn't always that way.

The top student in his Catholic grammar school class, Ben played guitar and, inspired by the adoration garnered by The Beatles, had a vocal band of his own. In sports, he was a Marksman first class rifleman in summer camp with numerous NRA medals to prove it. He also placed among the top swimmers in his age group in the New Jersey Amateur Athletic Union state championships three years running. He was a real charmer to boot, and girls were attracted to him from grade school on.

Because he had so noticeably excelled in everything he did, he was singled out by the local parish Monsignor who tried to encourage Ben's family to enroll him in the Seminary. Ben's father had other plans however, especially when the lanky young man received a full scholarship to New York City's prestigious St. Adolphus High School in Manhattan. St. Adolphus was the flagship of all Jesuit prep schools in the nation, and entrance was extremely competitive. Though there were many nationally recognized alumni that graduated from this school, Ben was the first student from his small upscale New Jersey hometown ever invited to attend.

Ben spent the next two years uneventfully studying, traveling to and from school, and representing St. Adolphus on two of its sports teams. With competitions taking place both during the week and on weekends, Ben's parents never attended these events since it was at least a two hour drive each way from their home. Besides, as one of the older children from a big family, Ben was sort of lost in the shuffle. His parents simply trusted that all was well within the hallowed halls of such a prestigious institution and that their son was receiving the best education possible.

Ben sipped his coffee and stared out the window to the scene seven floors below. He was stable and in a good place now, but three years earlier he was on the verge of suicide. Back then, he had pondered deeply the most effective way to end his life, and this thought plagued him for days at a time.

The suicidal thoughts became apparent as Ben was beaten down after years of trying just to have a chance at a modestly successful life. He had a lovely wife and an adult son to cherish and live for. But after getting laid off from his last post as a security guard, Ben joined the ranks of the unemployed and, sank further into the abyss of depression. He simply could not go on, unable to sleep and barely able to function. At the last moment, rather than ending his life, he sought his doctor's help and Ben entered the hospital without looking back on a Monday morning. As an inpatient, and in the succeeding months on an outpatient basis, Ben searched deeply for the real reasons for his failures and the inability to live up to the amazing potential he knew he'd had as a youth.

His reverie intruded by a chiming clock, Ben placed his coffee mug in the sink, grabbed his keys and headed for the door, turning off the television set as he did. Later that evening, Ben entered the double doors of the same, familiar local hospital that he had been in months before, and walked down a long, brightly lit corridor. Up a staircase and through a single door, he entered the meeting room where the local chapter of Rape and Abuse Victims of Clergy (RAVOC) was preparing to meet. The local chapter met on the fourth Wednesday of each month and Ben always arrived early but rarely spoke at these meetings.

He never discussed the sexual abuse he had suffered at the hands of the vaunted Headmaster at St. Adolphus. The abuse tainted his every move with guilt and shame and a tremendous sense of remorse. It made him doubt himself to the core. And though he had unlocked the terrible and shameful secret during his hospital stay, as much of a dedicated husband, father, and worker as he had become, Ben could not find release nor break the spell of the dark secret he kept hidden from everyone.

Leaders of RAVOC had written extensively about this topic and called it "Murder of the Soul," Ben discovered while reading a pamphlet he had been given while in the hospital. He came to his first RAVOC meeting while he was hospitalized and realized many others shared his dark, ugly secret and that he was right where he needed to be. Once released, he attended meetings regularly and became even more familiar with the organization.

Most of the member's stories were sickening and heart-wrenching. For instance, Gene, one of the main contributors of the local group, described his abuser, Father Ralph Bendazio, as a friendly and fun loving mentor. He spent a great deal of time enjoying basketball and other outings with the boys. But one by one, the youngsters would leave the basketball court, never to return. "I don't want to talk about it," they would say when asked why. However, they kept a noticeable distance from the priest.

At his family's encouragement, Gene often went with the kindly priest on weekend jaunts to Cape Cod and upstate New York. After a few months, the priest began tickling the young Gene. Tickling led to wrestling him to the ground or on a bed, and then finally, the older priest would hump Gene, until he, Bendazio, climaxed. Not knowing what was really going on, Gene blindly went along with it.

After weeks of this, Gene finally summoned up his courage and told his parents about the abuse declaring that he never wanted to see Father Bendazio again. Gene's father went up to the priest's supervising bishop to report the multiple incidents. The bishop responded, "Oh, is he still doing that?" It was swept under the rug and never mentioned again.

Father Bendazio never received any public discipline and remained in his post for many years to follow, working in close contact with other youngsters. Gene changed, virtually overnight, from a good student to a troubled youth, burying his shame, feelings of betrayal, and pain in alcohol and substance abuse. It wasn't until many years later, when that same priest was once again in the spotlight as an accused molester, that Gene made the courageous decision to come forward and confront his abuser. When he finally did he had a family and children of his own.

Gene sued the priest and the Church and won and the modest settlement awarded made it possible to start a new life. He was active in RAVOC for many of its fledgling years and became vital in the leadership of Ben's local group. As he attended more and more meetings, Ben recognized that sexual trauma can stay with the victim for life and cloud his or her every action. He was shocked to discover that countless thousands all over the world have been molested and abused by priests.

For some reason, tonight Ben found his voice and spoke up. He had been coming for several months and now felt comfortable. He didn't divulge all he had experienced, but provided the group with at least some of the details of what he had suffered. A hidden rage was slowly surfacing since his hospitalization, and Ben knew he must pursue this further, to a complete resolution. Speaking out was the first step, he realized. Ben never mentioned his perpetrator by name, but he opened up with Gene and the other attendees, shared his story, and asked for guidance.

At the meeting's end, Ben said goodbye to the other members and slipped out the doorway. Down the hallway, in the lobby waiting area, a television station was tuned to CNN.

"Fumata nera, black smoke!" noted the announcer.

Chapter 2
The Coming of Age

The College of Cardinals was in a state of tremendous disharmony and disarray with a great deal of jockeying for position by its members. After all, only the Pope himself was in charge of the Vatican Bank's secret billions, and no one else in the Church had that kind of authority or prestige. For that matter, no one else possessed the sheer power of being the spiritual leader of over a billion and a half people either...

The recently deceased Pope Boniface had had a rough time of it in the press as news broke of his brother's sheltering numerous predatory priests in a school for children in Frankfurt. The previous Pope's eyes were sunken and dark which gave him a sinister look. Pictures of him in his younger years giving a Nazi salute were present everywhere on the internet. Attempts to dispel the stories about his questionable past were mostly dispelled or ignored by the media. For many of the millions of Catholics, however, faith was blind, and denial was in their genetic makeup. Still, Catholics were leaving the Church in increasing numbers as wave after wave of scandal was uncovered, first in the U.S., then in Poland, Germany, Belgium, and Ireland as well. Even in Italy allegations were surfacing. Many people asked themselves just how long this could go on before the Vatican was held fully accountable and finally imploded.

As he listened to his voice mail, Ben smiled. It was from Barb Mackay, one of Ben's closest friends in RAVOC. Barb was active in media relations for the organization, facilitating numerous press releases and TV spots throughout Connecticut that called attention to the felonious and horrendous activities of numerous members of the clergy.

When she was 11, a priest had molested Barb in her own home before dinner with her family in the next room. He had been a trusted guest, and molested both Barb and her sister on several occasions. Like so many others, Barb buried the assault deep in her psyche, but it affected her every move. It went on this way for years, just as it had for Ben and thousands of other victims of assault by priests.

As the clergy abuse scandal in Boston was breaking, Barb heard it on the news while driving on the interstate. Overcome with emotion, she broke down and cried, forced to pull over. She just could no longer deny what had happened to her. Like so many others, Barb sought healing from psychotherapy and then found further healing and justice, not to mention a way to be part of the bigger picture, in the rooms of RAVOC. Barb used her media savvy and became very active in the media, petitioning for justice not just for herself but for all others who had been brutalized by this dark ordeal.

One story that she championed in particular was that of Denny Perry from a working class Boston neighborhood. At age 13, Denny was sodomized and murdered by his local parish priest. His limp, frozen corpse was found along the river the next morning by a couple strolling near a bridge behind the church.

Denny's perpetrator was moved from parish to parish in an attempt to cover up his deeds as well as his continuing criminal behavior. The police records of the Perry murder remained sealed for years and prosecutors would not cooperate with laymen and women seeking answers regarding the horrendous nature of this crime. The church held sway in these matters and used its enormous power to keep this affair quiet and out of the view of the public. A few months after Denny's death, the local Bishop sent a representative to the home of Denny's still grieving parents with a generous settlement offer, hoping to close the case and ensure the act remained secret. They were dumbfounded, unable to say a thing. Instead, Denny's father grabbed a baseball bat and chased the collared reverend to his Oldsmobile parked in the driveway. No police report was filed by the priest and the broken windshield was promptly replaced.

For several years, on the anniversary of his death, vigils were held in Denny's memory, and pictures were held up for the press to see. Accountability was demanded, but the parish's leaders and the diocese continued to ignore pleas for justice. Instead, they hid behind their priestly robes and vows of secrecy.

Ben emerged from his reverie and watched the news coverage. The election of the next Pope was still being discussed but Ben had only mild curiosity. Long ago he had exorcised the Church from his very core. As he watched, he noticed the throngs of people in the square and scoffed. To him, they were blind followers, gathered once more for their absurd and pretentious vigil in St. Peter's Square.

The divisive atmosphere of the Conclave was apparent to all within the locked room and spoke volumes of the deep schism in the Church both in Rome and around the globe. The deliberations went on for several more seemingly futile days, and though the Cardinals were not supposed to eat or sleep, they did both in defiance of canon law. Rather than exert the discipline and set the example of Christian Piety, most had grown spiritually flaccid, accustomed to living pompous and lavish lives.

By contrast, Ben was busy with several creative projects during this time period. Although he was unemployed and discouraged from looking for work given the intense competition from recent college grads and other younger workers, Ben kept busy. He created and ran a modestly popular internet website geared toward motivating and coaching others. Ad revenues helped him pay the bills and he planned the publication of an e-book on a related subject in a couple of month's time.

Disciplined in his work, Ben viewed everything he was involved in as a labor of love. Having finally recognized the source of his years of pain and suffering, Ben was taking his power back and was moving forward in his life as smoothly as possible. The only thing that gnawed at him was the injustice that he faced at that early age. A model student, gifted, talented, and blessed with a beautiful physique, he had been expected to go very far in his life.

After the assault, however, things changed and he thought of himself and more importantly, was treated by his formerly very proud family as a failure and a lackey. That prompted him to turn to drugs and booze. Substance abuse and deviant behavior were the ways he found to escape the ugliness of his past.

Once he hit bottom, however, Ben was ready to move forward. But until this was resolved, Ben could only go so far in his life. Justice was crucial, as was holding his perpetrator accountable for his actions. Ben didn't realize it at the time, but his quest for justice would be answered very soon. And when it was, the ramifications would reverberate around the globe.

In Rome, behind the granite walls, the College of Cardinals was shaking to its foundation, with members making blind deals and wild concessions in order to elect the next Pope.

"This body has grown old and tired and soon will die. I look for new blood if there is to be any hope at all for this organization in the years to come." Cardinal Micelli of Florence who had been one of the front-runners noted with a hint of melancholy.

Cardinal Reggio of Vatican City concurred and pled aloud to his colleagues: "If we do not agree soon on a new Vicar, well, the people are already restless. We are endangering ourselves and our very livelihoods by delaying any longer." His words persuaded them. In desperation and after further deliberation, for the first time in Vatican history, the college looked across the Atlantic and named a North American to be their leader.

White smoke danced its way heavenward as the world reveled in the prospect of a new Pope. The satellite news crews buzzed to life in St. Peter's Square. Television channels pre-empted regularly scheduled programming to break in with the news that after seventeen long and arduous days, a new Pope had finally been elected. Cable news anchors bandied about names with assurance and confidence, quite certain their "source" was accurate. It would not be long now until the new Pope made his way to the balcony to address the throngs below.

Inside the Papal chambers, Cardinal James Mayron of the Archdiocese of New York was trying hard not to gloat. There were those among his peers who were disgruntled at this choice and who felt that the selection of an American was entirely inappropriate. Others recognized that the dark cloud encompassing the whole of the Vatican was dangerous, and who better to assume the mantle than a leader who was seasoned in dealing with negative publicity, one who tangled constantly with the most formidable media outlets in the world, so the Cardinals rationalized. Despite misgivings, they unanimously selected Cardinal James Mayron of New York City to be the Vicar of Rome and of the entire Roman Catholic Church.

Deep in thought composing a new blog post, Ben was not listening to the television playing in the background. In the late afternoon, however, a change in the voice pattern of the anchor made him turn up the volume on the television set for what clearly was breaking news. He left his writing and turned his full attention to the news.

"Fumata Blanca! White smoke from the Vatican," said the anchor woman. "A new successor to St. Peter has been chosen and who that is will soon be known by the entire world. Stay tuned as we bring you the news live."

A news crawl below read: "Vatican sources confirm the selection of new Pope. Cardinal James Mayron from the Archdiocese of New York," and as he read the name and city on the news crawl, Ben felt like he had been gutted and tagged. He doubled over, then turned white as a wave of nausea engulfed him. His heart raced. His eyes remained transfixed on the screen, however, and he stood there, bent over, staring at the picture before him.

TV cameras worldwide were affixed to the balcony at St. Peter's Basilica and once the wave of nausea passed, Ben stood there unable to move. Minutes later, there was a rustle from behind the heavy red velvet curtains along the Papal Balcony and out emerged a grey-haired and somewhat gaunt figure garbed in the Roman Catholic Church's finest, white triregnum headdress and all. The new Pope stood there, grinning and waving to the crowds. The Bells throughout Vatican City rang out loudly, dimming the voices of television correspondents who were trying to provide on-the-scene reporting.

"*Urbi et orbi* – To the city and the world." This was the first vocal statement given by the new Pope as he shared his blessing with the multitudes.

Still motionless, eyes glued to the proceedings, Ben turned and ran to the bathroom where he dropped to his knees, hung his head over the toilet and vomited.

In St. Peter's Square, the crowds applauded wildly while behind the scenes the Cardinals scurried for power positions. Cardinal Silia from Naples scoffed at the idea of an American Pope and, obviously disgruntled, said to his colleagues: "This does not bode well for our Holy Church."

Cardinal Finnian from Dublin, on the other hand, welcomed the new Pope enthusiastically and prayed that it would signal a brand new beginning for the Church which had been racked with scandal after scandal for several decades now. "Perhaps we can put all this nefarious business behind us once and for all, and begin doing the Lord's work once again," he said to all nearby.

Wiping off spew and flushing the toilet, Ben drew himself up and braced himself; he knew his life had just changed forever. He made three phone calls in succession to unload the revelation prompted by the news of which he was now a part. The first call was to Barb Mackay.

"Slow down, Ben," Barb said into the phone, to an obviously highly agitated Ben Clancy. He'd always been so level-headed that she realized something significant must have happened to him.

"I am here for you no matter what," she said, hoping to calm him down. "Tell me what's going on."

"I don't know how to begin" Ben said, weakly.

"Just tell me what you need to say," replied Barb.

"Well, uhm, hey, this new Pope, ya know?" Ben said. "He's the man who assaulted me at St. Adolphus when I was a kid."

"O, my God, Ben! This is earth-shattering news! Please do me a favor and don't share this with anyone except those you can completely trust until we get solid advice. Don't do anything right now other than take care of yourself, all right?"

Barb hesitated, looking at her watch. Damn! She had an appointment she could not beg out of in 20 minutes!

"I wish I could come over, but I have to be somewhere in a few minutes. Let me see what I can do from here," she said, trying to give him encouragement. "In the meantime, are you going to be OK?"

Ben admitted that he was shocked by the news, but that he would maintain. Barb refused to hang up until she was sure Ben was okay. She promised to phone him later in the evening or early the next day. Ben was still very numb and had no clue what to do. He had two other confidantes to ring up, his sister Kelly and his brother Carl, a retired career diplomat who had served at embassies and consulates around the globe throughout his long career with the State Department.

Kelly was an energetic entrepreneur with street and business smarts. She managed to juggle several different projects simultaneously: she not only owned her own company, but she also worked for several large non-profit concerns as a media consultant. In the past, Kelly had even been very active in national politics and still had some connections there. More important than her resume, though, she and Ben were very close, and he trusted her implicitly.

As close as they were as siblings, Ben's reliance on his sister (and vice versa) went deeper than that. They were both highly artistic, kindred spirits, with a great deal of talent in their respective art forms and a great appreciation for culture in general. Ben was a gifted musician and writer, and Kelly was making a name for herself as a visual artist in her limited spare time.

Fresh off a reception featuring her work in a neighboring town, Kelly was stunned by Ben's news when he rang her up later that evening.

"Listen, Sis, I don't know any other way to say this, but the man who assaulted me and expelled me in high school is now the Pope," Ben said. "What the hell do I do with this?"

Kelly took a deep breath, hesitated a moment and said in a measured tone: "Ben, this is incredible, but you need to be calm. Keep this as quiet as you can for now and talk about it only with those you absolutely know you can trust. You know, the folks in – what's the name of your group?"

"RAVOC" Ben replied.

"Right, only talk to the leaders there that you are confident will keep this quiet for now, and see if they have any recommendations," she said. "I'll do some research from here, and you do the same. In the meantime, try to keep it together as much as you can and be sure to call Carl as well. He's very knowledgeable, might have some good connections to tap, and he's definitely on your side." Kelly encouraged Ben further and said she would do whatever she possibly could to see that justice comes to light.. Before they hung up, she hesitated, "and Ben?"

"Yeah, Kel?" his voice was growing smaller, she thought, and she was worried.

"Listen, if you need me, I can be on a flight up there tomorrow…" she said.

"You don't know how much that means to me, Sis," Ben said into the phone. His voice was breaking now. "I'll just take it a day at a time and you stay put for now and do your magic from there."

Ben called his brother Carl after reaching Kelly, but his phone went to voicemail. Rather than leave a detailed message, Ben just told him to give him a call, that it was important. Frustrated, Ben sank into a chair and thought about his situation. He realized he needed to wait for good information and for guidance from his closest "advisers."

He barely slept that night and woke up early, in a fog. He showered and poured himself a cup of coffee from a fresh pot, and sat down to think. "What the Fuck do I do now?" he wondered to himself. At 9 am, he rang Carl and was relieved to find he was there this time.

"Carl, I, I don't know where to begin. Did Kelly tell you the news?" Ben asked.

"No, but I was following press coverage of the Pope's election and heard the announcement last night." Carl said. "Sorry, I would have called you but we didn't get off the plane until late. "

"I did think it odd I didn't hear from you, but I forgot you were out west. We'll talk about your trip later, but for now, what do you think I should do?"

"You are in a very rare position, Ben," said Carl in a measured tone, "and you need to be very careful, very deliberate as to how you play this. Your whole life was damaged by this man and retribution is definitely in order and justified. Let me look into this from here and get back with you in a few hours. But first and foremost, are you doing okay right now?"

Ben told Carl that he was feeling very anxious and uptight. Carl listened patiently as Ben went on to describe that he felt he was in a deep, long tunnel and that he could not see the light at the end.

Carl said in a cautious yet warm manner: "Ben, this presents you with an opportunity to get beyond what happened to you, just realize that this is not going to be easy. Try to take it as calmly as you can and sit tight for now, okay?"

The two brothers agreed to speak in a few hours.

After they hung up the phone, Carl called a former vet he'd served with in the State Department overseas, Paul Adams, a lawyer in the New York area specializing in criminal law. He hadn't spoken to the man in years but felt sufficiently comfortable relating to him Ben's situation. What Paul told him took Carl by surprise.

Adams explained to Carl that because the Vatican is a Sovereign State, there is not much chance for a fair hearing regarding the Pope's past abuse of Ben in any court in the world. To make matters worse for Ben in terms of seeking justice, Paul explained that there's a Statute of Limitations on such crimes which would prevent Ben's seeking retribution.

"There is not much we can do on a prosecutorial level until that is overturned nationwide," Paul explained. "There are things that can be done in the press, however, but the emotional cost to your brother could be massive. These people will stop at nothing to protect their power."

"I have no doubt about that," Carl said.

"Have him write out his recollections of what took place as a sort of deposition and keep silent for now. I will see what I can do from here." Adams said. He was a realist, though, and knew that the Vatican was essentially above the law and had been since its formalization as a Sovereign entity with Mussolini in 1929.

After making further inquiries, Carl called his brother back a few hours later and related to him Paul Adams' advice. He said he would check on Ben the next day and that, between himself, Kelly, and Ben's RAVOC support system, they would help Ben come up with a suitable strategy.

"Don't let it get to you, okay, Ben?" Carl said, worry in his voice.

"I'll do my best," Ben said.

There are few factors in life as powerful as the "triggers" from the hidden memory of sexual abuse. Even talking about it launched Ben into an emotional spiral. He was on edge, very anxious and he had no clue of how to proceed. After what he'd already gone through in his life, part of him just wanted to crawl under a rock and drop it altogether. Most of him, actually. Why should he bother, he wondered?

After hearing Carl's news, Ben was disheartened and thought about taking off in his car and just driving until he could not drive any more. He had no urge to touch alcohol, but the fantasy of fleeing was strong. He loved the beach and could drive there. Off season, things would be very cheap and he could bring his guitar, walk along the shore and ponder his world.

Part of him, though, knew it was better to speak his truth. He had seen what a small band of men and women in RAVOC had done in less than 24 years. They had nearly brought the Roman Catholic Church to its knees as scandal after scandal had broken in the press, involving hundreds of thousands of children who had been raped and assaulted and scarred for life at the hands of members of an organization that considered itself all powerful and above the law. He wanted to believe that the Pope and those who covered up these actions were not untouchable in the court of public opinion.

Chapter 3
Bold Realization

After giving his circumstances more thought, Ben realized his best move was to do what Carl advised so he methodically went to work. He pulled out his notebook and cleared a place on his desk, poured himself a cup of coffee and set it down just as the phone rang. It was a friend checking in from RAVOC. Ben made up a brief excuse and got off the call quickly, then turned his attention to the paper. This was no time for small talk.

He stared blankly at the page for a time, willing himself back to that dark, painful place, waiting for his memory to take hold and whisper to him. He was concerned as to where to begin and started, innocuously enough, by writing about his arduous Catholic upbringing and some of his accomplishments as a youth. He described how he earned a full scholarship and attended St. Adolphus in New York for his first two years of high school. He wrote about his experiences there, excluding the abuse for now. His mind wandered back as he wrote, recalling that during his second year of high school, it was common knowledge among his classmates that he lived the farthest from school, with a round trip commute of about five hours each day. On top of that, he spent about three hours per day doing homework.

"I had no life at all!" he said to himself, clicking his pen in and out.

He went back to the paper and wrote that, in his sophomore year, he had to work very hard, especially in Latin, in which he was two points shy of passing at mid-year. To ensure he passed the final exam, his mother helped him each evening, ignoring all seven other siblings to drill Ben on verb tenses, pronouns and the like. It got to the point where even the pre-schoolers at home could count to ten in Latin, so used were they to hearing him recite the words.

His mind wandered back again to that Latin exam, his last for the year. He recalled that he took it with just five days left until summer vacation. After the test was over, he wrote, he went to the library with several others who were done with their exam. He explained on paper that they were all keyed up after completing the year end tests and he joined his fellow students laughing and telling jokes and in general letting off some much needed steam. They were all relieved to be done with their exams and were all talking slightly louder than normal.

Ben dropped his pen and stood up and stretched for a full minute or more. He went out to the porch with his guitar and played a brief staccato-like rhythm, the late afternoon breeze caressing his long dark hair. After a brief respite, he came back in and sat down again to continue.

"Perhaps my voice was louder than the others," he wrote, replaying the life-changing incident in his mind, "or maybe there was another reason entirely, but I was singled out to go and see the principle, Father James Mayron." He wrote steadily, the incident etched deeply in his mind.

"So you've been talking in the Library, eh? I'll bet you were making fun of Mrs. Marasco as well, weren't you?" Father Mayron sternly greeted the young Ben and slammed a book shut dropping it on his desk in an exercise of power and intimidation. Ben had always been a shy, well-behaved student, and never had to visit the principal's office before. He was scared shitless. Father Mayron, obviously enjoying his power over the meek student, rose and inspected the boy from head to toe, even looking from under his eyeglasses to get a closer look at the young man's face. After this scrutiny, the principal commanded Ben to come in for a special detention that last Saturday of the school year at 10 a.m.

Ben went home and an overwhelming sense of dread took over his entire body. He knew he'd catch hell from his parents who did not tolerate misconduct. And though the remainder of the week went by without incident, that Saturday in the middle of June, he caught the 191 bus at 7 a.m. bound for the city and his special detention. At 9:45, he silently opened the custodian's doors and meekly entered the concrete and marble building.

Ben felt completely alone as the sound of his footfalls carried eerily in the dimly lit passageway. He didn't know it yet, but this was the last time he would ever enter this building. The halls were dark and foreboding, and reluctantly, he climbed three flights of stairs, arriving at the headmaster's office where he knocked timidly. A gruff voice shouted "Come in!"

There were two rooms in the office quarters, the office, and an outer parlor with several tables, a red Persian rug and heavy gold brocade drapes that were pulled tightly shut. The light from outside struggled to enter in.

"Well, well, well, what have we here?" The headmaster fairly snarled. "If it isn't Mr. Ben Clancy, who likes to speak up when he isn't addressed! What do you have to say for yourself, Mr. Clancy?"

Ben stuttered, utterly powerless to reply. He tried to stammer out an excuse and apology all at once. The Rector impatiently held up his hand, scrutinizing the handsome youth as he had the other day. "This is very serious, young man, as this is a sacred institution," he said.

He allowed Ben's unease to grow, enjoying the power.

"What am I to do with you?"

Ben was utterly at a loss, completely subdued and powerless. The color drained from his face as he focused on the ticking of the grandfather clock. The remainder of his time in Father Mayron's office for Ben became surreal. From that moment on, clock chimes from the grandfather clock, Persian rugs, and gold drapes would be linked with the trauma that he was forced to endure over the next 90 minutes. The smell of Lectra Shave cologne still prompts an involuntary gag reflex in Ben to this day.

"Take off your shirt and drop your pants!" the priest snarled. Ben flashed him a questioning look but complied, obliged to do as he was told by the school's headmaster. He felt more vulnerable than he had ever felt before in his young life as Father Mayron walked all around Ben inspecting the naked youth all over. The priest then took a paddle nearly as large as a tennis racquet and ordered Ben to bend over the desk. The paddling lasted ten minutes or so with nearly a minute between each stroke. Ben's eyes remained locked forward, ironically on a copy of Warner Sallman's famous 1941 portrait, the Head of Christ, but he could hear the rustle of fabric behind him. And the Priest's breathing, which grew heavier. Ben didn't dare look back.

Eventually, the priest laid the paddle down on the table nearby and Ben waited, unable to breathe although his buttocks were stinging. He remained bent over, naked, totally vulnerable, waiting for the priest to tell him to dress. Suddenly the priest entered Ben from behind and raped him, grabbing the desk and surrounding the young boy's body with his hairy arms until he had finished gaining his pleasure. The pain was excruciating and Ben cried out several times, but knew there was none who could hear him. It stung and shocked Ben and he hated himself for taking it. After Mayron ejaculated, he moved away, grabbed a nearby tissue and cleaned himself off, straightened out his garments, and, without looking at the youth, told Ben to dress.

"If you speak one word of this to anyone, I will absolutely deny it. I will also make sure that you suffer very dire consequences indeed. Now get dressed and get out of my sight!" Mayron said in dismissal. It was clear that this was all about power and that in these black moments Ben had absolutely none.

Ben shrunk inside himself, dejectedly realizing that Mayron held all the cards. He was too stunned to feel hatred or any other emotion right now. He felt completely numb.

Ben walked into the hallway to the lavatory and after cleaning himself up, could not bear to look in the mirror. The damage was done. He weaved unsteadily down the halls and to the streets below, a changed and broken figure.

In his apartment in Connecticut, the adult Ben sank back in his favorite chair, reflecting for a moment before continuing to write. He wiped away tears, stood, and went back onto the porch with his guitar. As he played, he was able to process the memories into something he could grab hold of.

Back at his writing table, Ben picked up his pen again and wrote that the traumatized teenage Ben's next two weeks were spent in a stupor; a shock-like dream. In fact, it seemed more like years spent underground, vacuous. His brothers and sisters knew that something had happened to Ben, but he never spoke about the incident to anyone. Instead, he withdrew further and further, effectively isolating himself from his family.

Two weeks after the rape occurred, Ben received a notice in the mail expelling him from his beloved Prep School for poor academic performance. Though he had passed his Latin exam and brought up his grade to a 74, it was still not enough for him to pass for the year. It was his only failing grade and in his other classes, he did well. But as he found out almost 35 years later, he should have been able to attend summer school to make up the deficit with no stain on his record. With hindsight, he realized Mayron expelled him to silence him and in reality, it was a crime to cover a crime.

When he was expelled, Ben withdrew further from people than he already had. From here on in, he was a shell of the person he had been, merely going through the motions. All joy he felt, all desire to achieve, was ripped from his insides. Ben worked that summer as a lifeguard and mowed lawns and bussed tables on weekends and, in keeping so busy, he grew distant from the rest of the family. He always had a good work ethic, but lost was the promise and potential he had displayed in winning a berth to that elite school. And he hated himself.

With so many siblings, it was easy to hide. And since his dad worked such long hours he only saw him on weekends when chores needed to get done. His attitude grew surly and eventually, no one wanted to be around him any longer. He found alcohol and drugs as his only allies, a pattern of behavior that later ruined any chance he had of being successful in life.

On the surface he seemed happy-go-lucky, except when under the influence of booze or drugs. Then, Ben's dark side came to the fore. Still, he hid it well and was brilliant enough that he earned a scholarship to Notre Dame University, but lasted only one semester, getting drunk and stoned every day. At this time, he flat out did not care anymore. Life had very little meaning for him at this point. This pattern continued for nearly twenty years.

After dropping out of college, Ben had a multitude of jobs and was diagnosed with bi-polar disorder. Several stints in rehab proved ineffective and he still went back to booze and drugs. His family had no clue or understanding of what was really triggering him, but neither did he. At age 23, he knew he was an alcoholic, but he did what every good alcoholic should do, he drank more and more every day.

.

Chapter 4
New Beginnings

The aimless wandering and substance abuse went on for several years until one night when he was in his mid 30s. Ben received a serious beating by two rednecks at a club he worked in who pounded him in the face and on the back, breaking his jaw, nose, and cheekbone. On his back in the hospital for several days to recover, Ben had time to think about his life. Determined never to be so vulnerable again, Ben took up both Karate and Aikido as well as meditation. Through this, he was introduced to Eastern Philosophy and found in Buddhism a depth, richness, and reason that he just did not see in Western teachings.

Around this time Ben awoke one morning and looked at himself in the mirror. He knew he was throwing his whole life away and all his talents with it because of his reliance on booze and made a total commitment to get sober. He attended an Alcoholics Anonymous meeting the next night and never looked back. He did all that was asked of him in the program, made coffee, put out chairs, got a sponsor, shared at meetings, and spoke at many different locations including hospitals and prisons. He also sponsored many. Through AA and his Buddhist studies and meditation, Ben's spirituality grew and blossomed and he became a centered, compassionate, empathetic soul who deeply cared about others and his world.

He had begun playing his music again and took up writing, putting on paper his thoughts, observations, and experiences. He found it helped him work out his emotions. To support his Spartan lifestyle, Ben worked at various entry-level management jobs, never rising to the top, nor was he ever recognized for his strong work ethic and sharp mind.

Emotionally stronger than he had been in years, Ben met Jamie, a Korean American around this time. Her father had moved over after the Korean War and settled in the Northeast. He retired years later as partner in a couple of auto dealerships. Working hard from the day he arrived, he was able to provide a good life for his wife, daughter and two sons. He taught them all the value of integrity and good, honest effort.

Ben and Jamie both attended a Buddhist Philosophy meeting and connected right away. In the midst of a nasty divorce Jamie extricated herself, moved in with Ben, and became pregnant shortly thereafter. Brad was born healthy, strong, and beautiful and Ben vowed that he would protect them both with his life if necessary. Together, the trio became a typical family unit, with all of its bumps and scrapes and growing pains along the way.

Jamie, with her gentle eastern ways, aided in Ben's recovery as much as possible. But Ben was wracked by inner turmoil that would never be expunged until his childhood abuse was addressed. For many years, while they lived as man and wife, he buried it, too ashamed to reveal the experience, even with Jamie. Instead, he found it easier to avoid intimacy and keep her at a distance. Sometimes he just did not want to be touched at all and the strain in their marriage grew, cascading like an empty river.

In addition to a lack of intimacy, Ben's career path was unstable. He switched jobs several times over the course of a few years, in order to pursue his childhood dream of making it as a musician. Because of this, the couple struggled to make ends meet and raise Brad. By the time Brad was an adult, Ben's work instability grated on Jamie and things came to a head.

He would get laid off periodically or just simply quit due to a scheduling conflict or a temperamental outburst. Jamie grew more and more impatient. Realizing she was close to leaving him, Ben took a job at one of the state's largest employers to satisfy her. The position, however, required getting up at 3:30 each workday to start his duties on time. Lack of sleep led to a quick and serious depression and prompted thoughts of suicide. He spiraled downward rapidly. Ben just could not go on, couldn't take being beaten up by life anymore in low paying job after low paying job. He actually fantasized and came close to putting a nail through his heart with a nail gun he had in the garage. Instead, though, he called his doctor and broke down sobbing in an emergency meeting with him.

"You need a break," his doctor stated and Ben agreed, realizing the urgency of his situation. Doctor Manlow made arrangements for Ben to spend some healing time in the psychiatric ward of his local hospital. There, Ben surrendered. Although he had been sober now for almost 20 years, he was so beaten down, that both he and the staff realized there was something else eating away at him, something darker, more sinister and he could not bring it into the light just yet.

During the waning years of Ben's marriage, RAVOC and its members were making tremendous progress in the United States and Europe in exposing sexual predators, primarily from the ranks of the clergy. Ben had come across an article mentioning RAVOC several years before when allegations of clergy abuse had made a splash in the headlines of his home town newspaper. At that time, he had not faced his abuse yet, but the article had caught his eye all the same.

Boston found itself as the epicenter of the clergy abuse scandals in 1998. Investigative reports and trial transcripts showed that a corrupt Archbishop had known full well of the criminal abuse going on all around him. He did very little to stop it, other than shifting predator priests from parish to parish in order to cloak their activities and to keep things as quiet as possible. Few people ever suspected the wrongs these "men of God" perpetrated, born of a culture created centuries earlier that gave free reign to priests and their superiors. The ugly claims against the Boston Diocese rocked the nation and remained in the news for years and it was largely thanks to the tenacity of RAVOC and its heroic members.

While still in the hospital, in an environment of support and safety, Ben finally addressed the rape he had endured as a teen. With the help of the Doctor and others there, he acknowledged that he had been powerless to stop the abuse and that the ensuing years of decline and unfulfilled potential were through no fault of his own. He summoned the courage he needed to even broach the subject – in supervised sessions – with Jamie. He refused to discuss the details with her, but she did realize he had experienced a significant trauma that made it impossible to fully enjoy intimacy or give back to her in the way she deserved and needed. During these sessions they agreed that Ben would move out in order to spend time and "heal" himself.

He also decided, while in the safety of the hospital, to reach out to RAVOC and see if he could find healing within their midst. What he discovered in the months to come was a brutal yet compassionate honesty that empowered him and allowed him to make a fresh start. He learned from attending the group's meetings that what he suffered was a form of Post Traumatic Stress Disorder (PTSD). He had an epiphany when he realized that while he had been able to function in society for decades, the trauma and ensuing PTSD made it impossible for him to form healthy relationships or work successfully in any career until it was addressed.

Ben's stint in the psych ward was just what he needed to get his balance again. Before leaving the facility, he secured low-income housing, applied for and received notification he qualified for public assistance which supported him in very modest style. Brad picked him up from the hospital and drove him to Ben's new place which his son and wife had kindly furnished with hand-me-down items they found at the local Goodwill and other places. Determined to show that she was supportive and unwilling to end their marriage, Jamie was at the new place, cooking the traditional Korean dishes of Japchae, Bulgogi, and Kim Chee for them to share at Ben's folding card table in the center of the space that served both as the living room and dining room.

Ben attended RAVOC meetings regularly and became active in their lobbying efforts in New York State. Their current battle was to lobby for an elimination of the statue of limitations for civil cases of sexual abuse. The main reason, Ben learned, was that it could take years for the effects of trauma to surface, as it did in Ben's case. The powerful New York Catholic Arch Diocese resisted this lobbying effort with a vengeance and did what they could to influence the state's lawmakers. At the end of the legislative session, unfortunately, the church won. The bill died in committee.

Becoming more aware of his situation and the issue of clergy abuse and sexual predators in general, Ben wondered if the majority of people he knew who had substance abuse problems might be abuse victims themselves. Not necessarily of clergy, but abuse victims nonetheless. He was shocked when he discovered that the percentage of predators in the clergy is somewhere between 20 to 200 times greater than that of the rest of the population, but knew parents, relatives, babysitters, and others were often identified as abusers as well.

RAVOC members turned Ben on to more reading and one particular book suggested that the impact of sexual abuse was so profound it was considered as a form of psychological and spiritual death. The further Ben went into exploring this arena, the more he became enlightened to the truth of his own life. He had been robbed of his precious life, his potential, his future. And because of what he experienced that day in 1969 when he was raped and assaulted, a dark cloud loomed over his whole existence since then.

As he continued his research, Ben was able to find healing as well. Physically and mentally stronger, he wrote prolifically and dedicated himself to serving the highest causes he could. He kept up with both Buddhism and martial arts, and found them very healing for him, as he tried to strengthen and center himself.

Living solo for the first time in decades, Ben continued to write and enjoyed the freedom to play his guitar at the level he knew he was capable of. He had always loved cooking and began making great stews, breads, and other dishes he shared with Jamie, Brad and friends who came over to visit from time to time. The transition was easier than he would have thought and he began to flourish, reveling in his newfound independence and the healing of his psyche thanks in large part to RAVOC. It was the beginning of a whole new life.

Chapter 5
The Broad View

In his new apartment, Ben used his living room as a space to meditate, to write, as well as to workout. He was at the beginning of a whole new life, one that involved RAVOC more and more. He began to speak up more at RAVOC meetings and attended the Annual National Conference in Dallas, discovering firsthand the scope of the clergy rape and abuse crisis. The graphic stories he heard during that weekend instilled in him a stronger desire to expose the truth, along with an unquenchable thirst for justice for fellow victims.

Ben learned that with over 4200 known pedophiles among priests in the U.S., the problem in America was and is huge. Considering that each predator might have up to several hundred victims, the damage was unimaginable! In New York State alone, the estimated dollars lost in productivity for untreated victims of sexual abuse who later developed drug or alcohol problems or were otherwise incarcerated or institutionalized was in the hundreds of millions of dollars. The psychological and societal damage far exceeds that amount. What might have been if these lives had not been trampled on and destroyed is another fact to consider altogether. Ben came away from the conference ready to spread the message that this is a huge crime impacting all of humanity. In fact, it is one of society's worst ills. Unfortunately, he realized the Church and its hierarchy spend their resources covering up their errant clergy rather than addressing the widespread problem.

Back in October of 2010 Ben watched an hour-long CNN documentary entitled "What the Pope Knew," referring to the former Pope Boniface's knowledge of clergy abuse cases. According to the program, the Pope, in his role as Cardinal Arnold von Reichsinger, knew a great deal about all of these cases, but did almost nothing to improve the suffering of the victims. Instead of employing a rational, humanitarian approach, he focused on doctrine and dogma and maintaining secrecy within the Vatican, thus ignoring the problem. In doing so, rather than garnering support and appreciation, he created instead tremendous mistrust amongst even the most devout of practicing Catholics, but in particular, the general public.

Keepers of the Flame, the international organization that was formed to halt clergy abuse while shoring up the Church itself, distributed multiple copies of the CNN documentary in the hopes of precipitating an overhaul of Vatican affairs of State. The Keepers, unfortunately worked outside the inner circle of the Church's hierarchy, and were not strong enough to clean house properly. They were largely ignored by their own Bishops, even though some priests joined them in calling for reform.

Ben recalled reading about one courageous Arkansas priest who inadvertently led the call for change in the church. Father Reagan happened to mention to students in the high school religious education class he taught his belief that the Church should allow clergy to marry. He explained to the students, one of whom videotaped the lesson, that this would allow greater service and commitment by priests as they would have the knowledge of what family truly means and at the same time they would feel more complete, more whole. In his southern drawl, the priest also noted that the Pope was not infallible and was subject to making mistakes and actually was quite human, thus destroying the ivory tower myth that had enveloped the Vatican since its earliest days.   The incident made the national news because the student uploaded the video to YouTube, enraging school parents who were among the millions of viewers of the clip. In the end, this beloved priest was heavily censured by his Bishop for speaking his mind and forced into early retirement.

The leaders of RAVOC were hard at work lobbying for tougher laws and calling for prosecution of laws currently on the books. They were on the ground in nearly all 50 states. Their primary objective until now had been the removal of the statute of limitations for sexual assaults perpetrated on minors who did not or could not acknowledge and/or address the assault until years later, much as in Ben's case. Numerous attorneys around the country dropped all other cases in order to deal with this type of prosecutable offense and were involved in helping to push through new legislation. The focus was on the enormous amount of nearly irreparable damage visited upon the thousands of victims and its costs to society. In California and Delaware, the statute of limitations was eliminated temporarily and a window opened for civil suits for those abused even decades before. In California alone, this meant more than 300 sexual predators were named and brought to justice.

The financial awards were staggering and there were those who bemoaned this consequence and rallied around the Roman Catholic Church, making the argument that the Church generally served a good purpose. But the monumental harm visited on victims was no longer to be swept under the rug. Ben realized that the time had come. Justice must be the guiding force along with reason.

The former Pope had proven disastrous for the Church. Cardinal von Reichsinger, Pope Boniface, was notorious for being a rigid conservative with enormous influence in the Vatican. When he was elected to the Papacy, a lot of people around the world felt that this would deal an enormous blow to the Church after the hard-won global goodwill earned by the affable John Paul II.

Boniface had a dark history that would not escape him. For starters, he was identified as a member of the Hitler youth organization in the days of Nazi Germany, something he could never explain away thoroughly even after his election as Pope. In addition, he had been the Cardinal in charge of the Sacred Congregation for the Doctrine of the Faith, the CDF, which was the single remaining arm or wing of the Inquisition still in existence. The CDF wielded enormous power in the Church, and it was Boniface's aim to impose dogma rather than to alter behavior. During his reign as Pope, as stated earlier, it was revealed that he knew much more about the sex scandals than he let on, and did little or nothing to prevent or address them. At his death, the College of Cardinals – and hundreds of thousands of Catholics – breathed a sigh of relief, hoping for a positive change a new Pope might bring.

Founded in 1986 in Chicago by Brenda Lawson, a law clerk, and her partner and co-founder Daniel Callahan, the whole design of RAVOC was to foster justice for victims of sexual abuse from priests and nuns who had access to and influence over millions of young Catholics the world over. Both leaders had been sexually assaulted themselves and knew well the devastating effect of clergy abuse on the young. It drove them both to the legal profession and Brenda earned her J.D. not long after starting the organization. From the very start, RAVOC was born to right dreadful wrongs and to heal deep psycho/spiritual wounds. It viewed the long running history of abuse of power within the ranks of the Church to be entirely detrimental to society. Not a shred of good came out of that organization according to RAVOC's founders and many later members, and even the supposed good was tainted by a toxic poison. There was an intensity to members of RAVOC, yet at the same time there was a compelling wisdom that guided the organization's every move.

The founders picked up their first case in Milwaukee. A local priest, Father Sawyer from a parish in central Wisconsin, had molested scores of young deaf boys over a period of several decades, and left them scarred for life. Finally, one of the boys courageously stood up in his late 50s and named Sawyer as the man who had raped him. With Brenda and Daniel stepping in to champion the cause, the victim filed suit against the aging priest. Numerous other victims followed.

In the Milwaukee case, Brenda and Dan worked closely with Keepers of the Flame which, like RAVOC, was formed around this whole issue of clergy abuse and accountability. As Ben had learned earlier, "Keepers" had international reach and departed from RAVOC on its overarching mission -- to restructure the morals and ethics of the Catholic Church, while preserving the institution – whereas RAVOC would as soon see the church eradicated. Still, "Keepers" embraced the fledgling RAVOC as wounded warriors from among their own ranks and vice versa, and the two recognized that each would be a valuable ally in combating predatory clergy.

Ben spoke once at the Keeper's gathering in his home state, sharing his story in graphic detail. He also explained that he was no longer a Catholic but had become a Buddhist and was comfortable with his beliefs. In the end, he received a lot of support from the group, coupled with some intrusive questions from many who found his leaving the church inappropriate.

Ben shrugged off their disdain, feeling as many men and women of conscience did that if his country or organization was wrong he had a duty to speak out rather than blindly follow along with the status quo. Honesty demanded it. As for the Church, he had made his statement by leaving it, though his message was far from finished. For the members of the Keepers of the Flame who just didn't get it, well, Ben's friend and ally from RAVOC had a name for it. He called them Kool-Aid drinkers. They were the ones ready, willing and able to believe any lie that would soothe them and negate any real sense of dreaded self-responsibility from their system. He felt that most of those objecting to his message were still followers of an organization that no longer had any clear direction, having strayed far from its original mission.

Ben left the site of the speech encouraged by the large number of those present who came up to him afterwards saying they, too, had grown tired of the lies and wanted accountability. They had seen bishops flaunt their legal authority like distant manor lords over their flocks and command them to silence. These same bishops had turned up their noses at justice and grossly abused the rights of others, turning a deaf ear in almost every case for the sake of political expediency. Most were grievously selfish and self-absorbed.

All were acutely aware that they held a very real power over both their clergy and their congregation.

For centuries, in fact, ever since Constantine crowned Mitriades as the Pontifex Maximus, officials of the Roman Catholic Church held almost totalitarian power over entire nations, both religious and secular. Bishops, Cardinals and Popes had absolute power over all in their domain, and this included those in the rank and file of the organization, the priests and nuns, monks and deacons. The influence they wielded went well beyond the walls of the church to governing rulers as well. But the exploitation of power by these so-called Men of God throughout the centuries could only have been accomplished via a willing population. Thankfully, many within the Keepers of the Flame and the remainder of the Church community were willing no longer.

PART TWO

The Unfolding

Chapter 6
Bewilderment and Rage

The 24-hour news cycle replayed the scene in St. Peter's Square over and over again for several days, the airtime inundated with images of the crowds, white smoke, and news of the election of the new Pope after six long days of wrangling. The public appearance of the Catholic Church's first North American Pope, James A. Mayron, the former Cardinal from New York City, was aired on stations throughout the world. And talking heads wasted no time speculating about what this new Pope would mean for the church, how he'd rule, and whether his Papacy would benefit the church in the long run. Some news analysts even cynically speculated that he was elected solely to engage the North American Catholic population once again.

Back in the United States, his small town in New England was getting hammered with a winter snowstorm. Ben concluded writing down the events that had occurred nearly

40 years before, as his brother Carl had instructed him to do. After completing this task, he met with Carl and Paul Adams in New York. Paul was a former all-pro linebacker who later served in the Marines. Choosing to remain in government service after his four years, Adams gravitated toward the State Department's security unit, working his way up the ranks. Also retired, he and Carl remained in frequent contact.

When the trio met for lunch at an East Side deli they sketched out a framework that Ben was comfortable with. He would immediately be filing a lawsuit through a mutually agreed upon attorney. Adams would not be representing him for reasons of his own and for strategic purposes as well. They all agreed to wait and hear what Lawson and Callahan recommended before taking further action.

"Carl, I can't thank you enough," Ben said, somewhat choked up after Paul left. "He seems like a really sharp guy and definitely has his heart in the right place.

"Yeah, absolutely, he's been there. Listen, I've gotten involved in a new business venture in D.C., and will be kept busy with it for the next several weeks," Carl said as Ben drove him toward Penn Station. "Are you comfortable working primarily with Paul? You can definitely trust him."

Ben nodded his affirmation.

"Good, then just give me a heads up now and then to update me, okay Ben?"

"Absolutely," Ben said. "I appreciate your doing this for me, Carl!"

"Of course, bro," Carl said. "Listen, you take care of yourself and let me know if you need anything from me."

"Got it," Ben said.

The two said their goodbyes and Carl exited the car and headed into the station.

There was a tense energy surrounding Ben these days, and close friends that knew of his situation could only watch from a distance. Once he'd written his affidavit of the events, Ben started working on another larger version, this time, fictionalizing the characters to a slight degree and documenting the egregious history of the church as it related to abuses of power, sexual or otherwise. He knew that if things got to the point where a settlement was reached, the Vatican would likely want to secure his silence. Writing a fictionalized version, he decided, would be a good way to circumvent that restriction as well as help him process what he was experiencing without going absolutely nuts. He needed to get it all out and through this, he could accomplish just that.

Two days after the Pope's election, Ben met with the core team of his local RAVOC group. There he laid out his charge: The man who had been elected leader of the Catholic Church in Rome was guilty of crimes against humanity in the form of rape and sodomy against at least one young, innocent boy. There might be other victims, Ben speculated, given the new Pope's former position as head of an all-boy's school and his penchant for wielding that power under intimidating circumstances.

With formal allegation in hand and Ben's willingness to go public with the charge, the advocacy team went into action immediately. Barb put in a conference call to Lawson and Callahan out in Chicago and spent a solid hour on the phone with them. After reacting briefly to the initial shock, Dan recommended that Ben get in touch with Jerry Sanders, a nationally prominent attorney from Chicago who had been head litigator on several international cases involving clergy abuse.

RAVOC was in full action mode now. Brenda and Dan put out discreet feelers in the Midwest about the Pope's background, and Barb did the same on the East Coast. They made Ben aware of the multitude of different possible outcomes and consequences awaiting him if he did in fact go public with his charge.

When he was younger, Ben had had a strong sense that he was destined for something big. That feeling had disappeared when he was abused and expelled from St. Adolphus and from then on until his recent acknowledgement of the rape, he lived with self-loathing and ignominy. He never guessed that that incident might be the trigger that would bring his fate and destiny full circle, but on reflecting, it made perfect sense. If it were up to him though, this never would have happened, since this event had scarred his every action and darkened his every step for so many years.

Back in his apartment, energized from the meeting, Ben poured a cup of coffee and began to work. His pen moved effortlessly across page after page as he reworked his affidavit, recalling in even greater detail the event that took place almost 40 years ago. The meeting with Carl and Paul had given him the courage to go back there, to that very dark place, and write in gut-wrenching honesty all the details of his trauma.

Ben's sister Kelly was busy as well, researching the background of the former Headmaster, James Mayron. After his tenure at St. Adolphus, Mayron was promoted to the presidency of Fordham University in 1974, she learned. He then went on to become Archbishop of New York in 1987 and was appointed Cardinal four years later. Like Boniface, Mayron was known as a hardliner, far more interested in static dogma than growing the church through more open means. He reveled in his own pomp and wealth like so many in power in the Catholic Church.

Kelly read with interest old news articles about Mayron. She discovered that in 1998 accusations of sexual assault against several of the Bishops in his archdiocese surfaced, and this was followed by his subsequent relocation to Rome. Instead of a public dressing down, she observed wryly, Mayron was rewarded by being named the Vatican Secretary of State, a first for an American.

Cardinal Von Reichsinger was head of public relations for the Vatican at the time and found himself continually on the defensive as the Church was increasingly under International scrutiny on a number of fronts. Mayron served directly under the previous Pope during those years, skillfully putting out public relations fires, while drawing attention to the church's good acts. Despite the attempts at good, solid P.R. work, "Vatican, Inc," Kelly thought, was guilty of some very serious wrongdoings and many in the international community were aware of it.

As she delved further, Kelly came across the details of the 1929 decree by Mussolini that enabled Vatican City to become a Sovereign State. She realized that for centuries before that, the Vatican had often acted as a supreme power above the law and documentation showed that this attitude prevailed up until the present time. Kelly wondered if this spiritual elitism would soon be tested, thanks to her courageous brother and those working with him, as well as many other passionate people from around the world.

Ben continued to record the incident. He challenged himself to remember every detail surrounding his abuse and its resultant aftermath. In checking one very important point, he called the St. Adolphus High School office and discovered that his expulsion had been a departure from stated policy and never should have happened. Although he had marginally failed Latin for the year, a single Summer school class would have made up the deficiency. These classes were offered there since the school's foundation in 1914 for just such cases.

Expulsion was only warranted if two or more classes resulted in failure.

Later, while going for a run, he processed this new information and the wrong that had been done him. It amounted to this, Ben thought: He had been a golden child, winning a full scholarship to the most elite Catholic prep school in the nation. The good headmaster had desired and sexually molested Ben, taking advantage of the vulnerable, eager-to-please high achiever. Guilt, disgust, and fear of discovery led the priest to take the drastic and unprecedented measure of expelling Ben. And Ben's parents, the good Catholics they were, did not think to question the Headmaster's decision or motives. Ben was the fall guy for the priest's lust and lack of self-control and IT.DESTROYED. HIS.LIFE.

After many years of living under a dark cloud, he was ready to find liberation from the damning after-effects of the abuse and ensuing expulsion. Once the magnitude of it all sunk in, Ben slowly found the energy and desire to fight back. He wanted nothing more than to regain his power and live the rest of his life with the dignity and respect he so richly deserved.

His immediate concern was finishing his written testimony. He would then move on to the next step with the help of his seasoned friends within RAVOC. His inner self-loathing had been replaced by a multitude of emotions: anger, determination, fear. Fear of what he had discovered in this new pope, and fear for what that knowledge could do to him. Ben made a vow to himself right then as he cooled down from his run. He promised himself that he'd hold Mayron accountable and not get swayed by circumstances beyond his control if he could help it. Little did he know how that vow would come into play again and again in the next few weeks.

Chapter 7
The High Cost of Freedom

Barb called Ben just before he had completed writing his statement, wanting to know how he was holding out emotionally. Her message was brief but unconditionally loving and supportive. They agreed that Barb would relate Ben's current status to the co-founders of RAVOC and see if they had identified any other derogatory information about the Pope through their sources and come up with a recommended course of action. To Ben and Barb's minds, their next action would be the first step in a very public offensive launched against the Vatican. They knew they had to be careful, ensuring there were no missteps.

Carl checked in to make sure Ben was alright as well and to see if he had heard from Paul. Two years older then Ben, Carl knew full well of Ben's successful fight over alcohol and drugs and low self esteem. Although he was convinced that Ben would overcome this as well, Carl knew the situation was very different. This was the putrid source of all Ben's difficulties. His brother was suffering from PTSD due to the trauma of the sexual abuse that had occurred almost 40 years before. It was now more than likely rekindled by this sick perverted excuse of a man elected as Pope. An avowed agnostic, Carl shook his head in disbelief at the decay and dysfunction of that errant empire.

After speaking to Ben, though, Carl was relieved to discover that the trauma itself and the memory that was so deeply imbedded within him did not seem to destabilize Ben at this point. If anything, it seemed to redirect him, and motivate him with a newfound sense of purpose. Carl was grateful to RAVOC for helping Ben in the recent past as he worked his way through the realization and acknowledgement of the trauma he'd experienced. Clearly, Ben was now ready to deal with this. But Carl wondered if Ben realized the magnitude of the full-out assault against his character he predicted the church would launch against Ben not so far down the road. He knew the Church would never allow this to go public without a major battle, either legally decided or played out in the dark corners of the underworld where the Church could maneuver in secret.

After speaking to his close allies, Ben recognized he had a genuine need for counseling specific to the sexual trauma he had undergone. He paid a visit to a local counseling center mainly for younger people. That was of no concern to him, he knew he needed the help. During his first session and over several subsequent sessions, he cried at the deep loss he had suffered. He had effectively lost his whole life, but he was now learning he could get it back with effort, time and healing. Shawna, his therapist, had a compassionate smile and a box of Kleenex waiting for him each time they met. She helped him work through the many layers of negativity, self-loathing, distrust and failure he had encountered in his life going back to that fateful Saturday.

After his first session with the trauma center, he was filled with a calm resolve. He returned home, sat down with a cup of coffee and read through the recently completed written testimony. He read it word for word for the hundredth time, and though four decades had passed, the encounter remained still vivid in his mind. He made several copies, but did not show the document to anyone just yet. He wished to present the first copy to someone very important in his youth and because it was getting dark, made plans to do just that on the following day.

His usual morning routine of caffeine and meditation completed, Ben set his GPS coordinates and followed the kindly sounding digital voice to St. Anselm's cemetery in Meriden, Connecticut. It was mid March and the sun was breaking through the high clouds. When he had parked his car, he took a deep breath and let out a sigh. He placed a copy of the document in a thin metal canister and proceeded up the hill to his family's gravesite. When he got there he chanted his Buddhist chant and breathing deeply, embraced the silence for a very still moment. Exhaling, he knelt down to score the earth in a spot by his mothers' headstone and placed the canister in the crevice he formed there. He then covered the spot and put the grass back where it had been, tamping it down as he spoke very softly, looking at the headstone.

"Mom, you were wrong about all of this. You could have prevented what happened, but you didn't because you were too blind," Ben said softly. "Even after it happened, I couldn't turn to you because you wouldn't have believed me. Instead you thought I was like a lost sheep, someone who had taken a wrong turn. Well, there was a reason for that, and it's all in there," pointing toward the cylinder he had just buried.

"I know you meant well, and I can only hope you are at peace. There is a Gypsy saying that is a favorite of mine and it is 'Patshiv Tumenge Romale'. It means 'There are lies more believable than truth'. I don't hold you accountable, you were lied to along with the rest of the world. What we need now is a Revolution of Honesty. Wish me luck, Mom, I now know what I have to do. Be at Peace".

Shaking as he concluded his visit, Ben stared in silence for a few moments at the earth where his mother was buried then stood a little taller, and braced himself, resolved to do what he must. He started back to his car at first slowly, deep in thought. He then picked up speed and sprinted the last 50 yards or so. He unlocked his car door and got in inside, gazing at himself in the mirror. The face that stared back was confident and assured. He took a deep breath, knowing that his next sequence of actions would drop him dead center into a snake pit. He started the car and drove back to his apartment. When he got there, he called Barb.

"How are you?" she asked, a worried edge to her voice.

"I'm good" he said. "I am now ready to do whatever I need to. I'd like to speak with Brenda Lawson and Dan Callahan. I really could use some sound advice. The written testimony is done and I am ready for the next phase."

Barb reassured him quickly, "Perfect. They were eager to talk to you and suggested you call as soon as possible. Just let me know what you decide after you speak to them, okay Ben?"

"I'll call them in a minute," Ben answered and said goodbye. Before dialing, he gathered his thoughts and punched in the number for RAVOC's Chicago Headquarters. Brenda and Dan were in court so he left a voicemail message for Brenda.

"Brenda, this is Ben Clancy from Connecticut's RAVOC. You know of my case through Barb McKay and I'm anxious to discuss it with you and Dan. Please call me when you can as I very much need your input on this." He left his telephone number and disconnected.

Over a quiet dinner alone, Ben kept thinking of the expression, "All roads lead to Rome." How ironic, he thought. He was deep in contemplation when the phone rang. It was Brenda Lawson.

Ben knew something of her story. How she had been molested by a priest as an 11-year-old in a Catholic school in Detroit back in the seventies. He knew how cold she could be when dealing with the Church and any authority that smelled of corruption, but he also knew that she could be kind and protective towards survivors. He understood her emotions and appreciated them. He saw her in action as they lobbied the New York State Assembly in Albany, New York on behalf of RAVOC. As a neophyte to all that, he just stood back and watched her, amazed at her skill, competence and passion.

"Hello, Ben?" Her voice was strong and commanding.

"This is Ben ... Brenda?"

"Yes it is," she replied.

"Can I call you back on my land line? I would feel more secure," Ben said.

"Of course" She said, "Let me give you my home number."

They hung up and Ben immediately called her back.

After a short exchange of greetings, Ben got to the point. He filled her in on the written testimony he had completed and asked her advice on what to do next. Brenda suggested that Ben contact Jeff Sanders, a Chicago-based attorney who had dealt with multiple cases of clergy abuse and who was also versed in International Law. Brenda said that she, with

Ben's permission of course, would contact Attorney Sanders first thing in the morning to fill him in as best she could on the seriousness of Ben's case. Before hanging up the phone, Brenda hesitated.

"Oh, and Ben?"

"Yes?"

"Please know you have my full support, and that of Dan Callahan and the entire RAVOC organization. This is going to take all the energy, resources and power we have, but we're with you every step of the way. I want you to remember that, okay?"

"Thanks Brenda, that means a lot to me."

At bedtime, Ben tried to lie down and get some sleep but he was too keyed up. He knew he'd taken a huge step and in doing so was opening up a Pandora's Box of God-knows-what. His imagination went overboard and for most of the night, he kept one eye open in case "they," should try to enter. He tried to laugh off his fears, but found he couldn't. He had heard stories of how unscrupulous the Vatican could be, and how enmeshed with the Mafia it was.

Ben got up around 1 a.m. and flipped the TV on, but there was nothing worth watching. Sitting in the darkness, he reviewed the events of the preceding few days as a growing sense of unease took over. Corny as it sounded, he was almost afraid for his life now. Still, he knew he had to speak out and he looked forward to the next piece of the equation fitting into place, as he continued in his search for equilibrium and justice.

Ben felt alone, very alone. But he consoled himself realizing that he had the support of his family and friends, and RAVOC. And from here on in, he would try to incorporate his Buddhist teachings and simply follow the path, letting go of any desire to control the events that were about to unfold. Wryly, he thought, he couldn't control those events even if he wanted to.   The acceptance of this helped him relax and finally fall asleep.

Chapter 8
The Unfolding

Ben awoke at 7:30 a.m. from a dream in which he saw the sun, brilliant and aglow, lighting up a dark and dank passageway filled with millions of people, and he understood the metaphor. He felt assured that all was going to be well one day, and that all was well even now that history was unraveling. He felt strongly that he had a special role to play in this unfolding drama. He poured a fresh cup of coffee and glanced at his schedule for the day. The only pressing thing he had going on was his mid morning call to the attorney Jerry Sanders. He meditated for an hour or so then ate breakfast, showered, brushed his teeth and tidied up his place. He figured he would call Sanders around 10 a.m. Central time. By now, Ben understood the stakes very well, and in a way he had been waiting for this moment for a lifetime. His anxiety mounted all morning though as he tried to busy himself by writing a blog post. He watched the clock and moved around intently, ready to spring, like a panther.

Finally, at 11 a.m., he dialed the attorney's number hands shaking slightly. "Sanders and Johnson", the voice at the other end of the line answered. Ben announced who he was and was told by the administrative assistant that Jerry Sanders would be in court all day, but that he would be checking his calls throughout. Could she take a message?

"Yes," Ben answered. His left his name and phone number with the secretary and explained that Brenda Lawson from RAVOC recommended he speak with attorney Sanders. He was assured that Sanders would get back with him within a day or so.

Somewhat relieved, but also somewhat let down, Ben went about the rest of his day, remaining very anxious though he tried to calm himself with meditation, music and a walk. He also kept busy doing several errands and made calls to his main three contacts: Barb, Carl and Kelly. That evening, he had a dinner date with Jamie.

At dinner, he told her a little about the unfolding events and she encouraged him to be calm and simply tell his story. They both knew how the abuse had hurt their relationship. Ben had grown isolated and irritable before his breakdown and she, Jamie, just couldn't take it anymore. They occasionally discussed the possibility of getting back together again after the divorce, but both wisely agreed now was not the time. With Ben facing all he was indeed facing, it was imperative for him to be as clear-minded and focused as he could in order to allow the healing process to take hold.

Driving her home in the car, Jamie merely said, "You have something very important going on here. I will definitely chant for you"

Ben wanted to tell her that he had been a faithful, kind and loving man from the very beginning, but with the surfacing up of PTSD and the cloud that had been over him, that he had only been half a man and that she deserved better. After dropping her off, he drove around for a time, reflecting on their failed marriage and his flawed life. Turning into his apartment parking lot, he reiterated his vow to himself to take his power back and finally live up to his full potential, no matter that he was getting old. Armed with newfound confidence, Ben knew he could do it, too!

He filled his evening by watching television and then meditated in silence in the semi-darkness as he did each night. He went to bed less tense than the night before and actually got a good night's sleep, waking up around 9 a.m. Greeted by a cold, cloudless morning, he showered, shaved and dressed and then sat at his desk contemplating his hoped-for phone call with Attorney Sanders.

Ben's heart jumped when the phone rang around 10:30 a.m. It was not the attorney, but a friend who wanted to meet for coffee and the disappointment was evident in Ben's shrug and in his voice. Ben rarely blew people off and was always generous with his time, but on this occasion he explained that he couldn't meet as he had some major issues to deal with.

Two hours later, the phone rang. It was Sander's secretary asking for Ben. She put him on hold and a few minutes later Sanders came on the line.

"Ben Clancy?" Sanders asked.

"Yes, it is." Ben answered.

"I spoke with Brenda Lawson the other night and she gave me an overview of your case. I understand you have been through a tremendous amount. Can we go over the details now?" The attorney asked. His voice was terse and businesslike. Still, there was an underlying sincerity to the tone and Ben got the feeling that he could trust the lawyer.

"Yes, we can." Ben replied.

"Good," said the attorney.

Over the next hour and a half Ben related the details of the abuse, how it occurred, when and with whom.

"Were there any witnesses present?" Sanders interrupted at one point. He asked several more pointed questions after which the sharp attorney explored something Ben had never considered before. He asked Ben if it were a setup.

"I'm sorry, I-I'm not sure what you mean, sir?" Ben replied.

"Was there a 'point' person in the library who deliberately picked out boys for the headmaster and then had them sent down to him?" The attorney asked. "I've seen this kind of behavior before, this m.o. you know, and it's disgusting and it really angers me."

At that moment, Ben's heart rate climbed exponentially. "Holy shit" he thought to himself. "I never thought about that," he exclaimed aloud to Sanders. "I honestly have no idea and no recollection of who sent me to Father Mayron for the punishment, I'm sorry."

"Don't you find it curious that you were sent down to the headmaster instead of to the rector in charge of the school's discipline?" Sanders asked.

"That ... never occurred to me," Ben replied, wonder in his voice. "I was so worried about getting in trouble, see."

"And was it the usual practice for the school to discipline students on a Saturday when no one else was to be present?"

"Back then, Saturday detention was rare but it did occur," Ben said, shrugging. "My younger brother, who went to the hometown Catholic school had to go in on Saturdays occasionally. They'd, you know, have them clean the blackboards, empty trash, stuff like that."

Sanders then went over the description of the abuse itself, clarifying issues and details. By the time they got through Sander's questions, Ben was spent. Sanders then summarized his thoughts for Ben, choosing his words very carefully.

"Ben, this is a difficult case. First of all, it happened nearly 40 years ago and second of all, the priest who assaulted you is now the Pope. The Vatican is notorious for never answering to outside civil or criminal complaints or suits," Sanders explained. "And since this would be filed in the States, naming St. Adolphus High School... In short, the Vatican is a Sovereign State, and does not have to comply."

Sanders let that news digest.

"I see," Ben answered.

"However, because the alleged crime took place here in the United States, there may be something we can do. Do not discuss this with anyone except those closest to you," Sanders instructed.

"I won't, sir," Ben said.

"I'll be in New York City next Wednesday, is it possible for you to meet me then?" Sanders asked. "I share an office there with an old friend and colleague and I'd like for us to discuss this in person if you can come in?"

Ben agreed to the meeting without hesitation.

"In the meantime," the attorney went on, allowing Ben time to collect his thoughts, "My secretary, Alicia, will email you some paperwork to fill out. Try to get it done as quickly and thoroughly as you can and send it back to me   You do have a computer, I suppose?" he asked.

"Yes, I do," said Ben. "And as a matter of fact, I recently typed up a written testimony about the account. You know, describing it in detail. I don't know if you can use it but--"

"That will be useful," Sanders said, cutting him off. "I'd like for you to send it to my Secretary, who I'll put on in a moment so she can give you my e-mail address. She'll also give you details of our meeting – I'll have her set it up for early afternoon since you're coming in from … Connecticut, right? Can we do this?"

Ben agreed wholeheartedly, placing his trust in this man he had never met. He waited on the line as directed and when Alicia picked up the phone he gave her his contact information and in turn took the e-mail address she shared with him. Once he disconnected, he drafted an e-mail and attached the affidavit he had prepared and sent it on its way to Sanders' office.

Relieved that this part was over, Ben had lunch and read. He went for a long walk in the park to clear his head. He was in for the fight of his life and he knew it. The first blood had been drawn four decades earlier and he was now, finally, strong enough and ready to respond.

Returning from his walk, he called Barb, Carl, then Kelly, and related to each the details of his conversation with the attorney. He admitted to each that he was an emotional basket case reliving all of this. They all reassured him of the rightness of his actions and that he would be okay. Kelly repeated her offer to come up or fly him down for a brief visit. He thought about her offer for a while but called her back and told her he'd rather stay put and could get by as long as he knew that she could be reached.

In his down time, Ben began writing feverishly, working on his fictional treatise of what had happened to him and thousands of others. He began by sketching some of the history of the Roman Catholic Church and the words came effortlessly as if the pen had a mind of its own. Over the years, he had studied countless volumes on the Western

World and felt it was now time for him to spill his heart and soul out on paper. He wrote 14 pages the first day, and another 12 on the second. He was determined to complete this work which he didn't have a title for yet, by the following autumn. He pondered calling the work "A Dangerous Truth", and then went back to work in solitude pushing himself ever harder.

As a youth, Ben scored in the gifted range, and in eighth grade read at the level of a college senior. That's how he landed on St. Adolphus' radar where, to even gain entry, students had to show a record of highest achievement from school grades, standardized and IQ test scores, and personal interviews. After the abuse, Ben's downward spiral was stark and those who never knew him pre-attack were stunned to discover how intelligent, well-read and well-spoken he was, given his negative demeanor.

Moving beyond the scars that he had incurred, Ben wanted his life back and realized that this was his time to recapture it. He wanted his life to have meaning, deep and powerful, rich and true. He vowed, as he had several times recently, that he would do whatever it took to call out his attacker publicly and reclaim his integrity. He was ready to go balls to the wall, all out, even if it meant disclosing his ugly secret. He was keenly aware that by doing so, he'd finally be set free.

As strong as he was in the literary field, Ben was also an accomplished guitarist as well and played every day even if just for a few minutes to tune himself up. He also played when tense, as a form of supreme release. One of his closest friends noted that his playing was on the lines of classical Spanish style. Ben thought of his unique style as 'fusion,' but either way, he played as though performing songs to the universe. He was adept at improvisation and it helped him dramatically with his songwriting. Though never commercially successful, he still had a loyal fanbase in the Northeast of people drawn to his music.

Outside on his porch, he reflected on his life at this juncture, fingering his guitar as he did. Although he was reopening painful and deeply buried wounds that had finally come to the surface, he still had a strong spiritual outlook. Disdaining the dogma of organized Western religion, Ben recalled a saying from one of his 12-step meetings, "Religion is for people who don't want to go to Hell, and spirituality is for those who have already been there!" His Buddhist studies taught him that heaven and hell were internal worlds. The trick was to not get swayed by the current of emotions that sometimes gets so strong as to pull one under. Right now, he clung to that lesson as his emotions were in overdrive, reaching a height that almost frightened him. He knew that all that was happening to and around him was occurring for a reason. He prayed that the entire affair would have a good resolution.

Chapter 9
The Waiting

Ben did a lot of working out over the next few days until his appointment with Attorney Sanders. He hadn't been into the Karate dojo in ages and it felt very good to get back to it, since it released a lot of the tension he felt. The two brothers that owned the dojo were both high ranking black belts and were glad to see him. In addition to the Karate workouts, Jamie joined him for pleasant walks through the late season snowfalls and he met up with Brad and Brad's co-workers for some pickup basketball where Ben's still potent hook shots and sharp sense of humor made him a popular team selection.

Right around that time, he also met with Paul Adams at a quaint New York eatery which still had Valentine's décor up. The two reviewed his written deposition before he emailed it to Sanders. Adams refused to take a retainer for advising Ben, simply explaining he was glad to do it. His sharp eye caught a couple of points he thought Ben might want to elaborate on and the two of them discussed Ben's unfolding manuscript as well. Paul was curious and, with friends in the publishing industry, wanted to see if he could help Ben broker a deal on this. They both had their personal reasons for shining light on the sex abuse scandals and Paul himself was very well aware of the corruption in the Vatican, hence he viewed the book as serving two aims at once.

Once Ben returned home, with Paul's recommendations fresh in his mind, he tweaked the deposition he had written immediately after Mayron was selected as Pope. Paul had given him some good suggestions and had reminded Ben of a couple of points he had left out that the pair thought very important to include. The completed document was well over fifty pages including revisions, and Ben put it together in just a few days. He hoped this affidavit would be useful to his case, but regardless, the words just flooded forth like a surging river when he drafted it and he knew instinctively that the process was crucial for his healing.

On Friday, Attorney Sanders' secretary called him to confirm the date, time and place they were to meet in New York City the follow week. She also let him know that she had received the affidavit he'd sent over. He held off sending it until after incorporating the revisions recommended by Paul who was fast becoming a trusted mentor to Ben.

By Saturday he was confident that the manuscript he was churning out, a departure from his testimony, had some real-world value. Paul had wholeheartedly agreed and encouraged him in this, and he discussed its publication with Kelly, who had worked for several years in the publishing industry. The brother and sister team discussed the merits of shopping the manuscript around to major publishing houses. They agreed that Kelly would make a few discreet inquiries and if anything interesting came along, they would run it by Paul for advice.

Ben's overarching motivation, he made clear to Kelly, was not to get rich, but to get the information out into the public. He wanted it outside the media filter and in a manner, keep it fictional if necessary, which would reach a broader audience and hopefully, provoke them to reflect on the church's misdeeds in a way straight non-fiction might be unable to. Kelly knew this and was totally on board. She'd seen her brother suffer tremendously over the years, and understood the importance of his message. Aside from that, she really respected his intellect and overall approach.

Though events in his life were unfolding rapidly and dramatically, Ben had reached a place of calmness, clarity and insight, thanks to his Buddhist studies. He knew he was surrounded by friends and family he could trust. He was also about to expose the Roman Catholic Church's highest ranking official and possessed a truth so powerful that he could not and would not remain silent.

On Tuesday night before his meeting with the attorney, Ben laid out his clothes and meditated. He rose early on Wednesday, had coffee and chanted quietly for a few minutes. Then he gathered his legal brief and his copy of the affidavit and headed out the door to the elevator. Exiting in the lobby, he walked briskly toward his car, breathing deeply the cool crisp air of early April in New England.

Ben drove in silence the two plus hours to New York City, never once turning on the radio. He needed his thoughts clear and sharp. He got off Route 84 onto the winding Saw Mill River Parkway and enjoyed the ride. Traffic was fairly light as rush hour was long over. Approaching Manhattan, he exited off the West Side Drive in midtown. There, the sense of calm left him and he felt his blood pressure soar as he crossed over

11th all the way down to 5th Avenue, heading south to the lower East Side. He parked in a garage just a few blocks from Sanders' office and walked the remaining distance, focused on his pending meeting.

As Ben sat waiting in the anteroom, Attorney Sanders came out and introduced himself, escorting his client to the conference room. Another man, presumably an attorney as well, was already seated along one side of the polished mahogany conference table, along with a legal secretary set to take notes.

Because the stakes were so high, Ben was anxious, but reminded himself that these were the good guys. Sanders introduced his colleague, Attorney O'Donnell as Ben shook their hands and they all took their seats. After offering Ben coffee from a caddy in the center of the table, which he politely refused, Attorney Sanders was the first to speak. He was shorter than Ben expected, but dressed in a tailored suit with tight suspenders, and looked very impressive indeed.

"Ben, we received the document you emailed us detailing what happened at St. Adolphus in '69. Technically it's not an affidavit, but more a testimony. That's beside the point. It was well-written and detailed, but I do have a few questions to ask you and my co-counsel, Attorney O'Donnell may have some for you as well. Please make yourself comfortable, though I know how disturbing reliving this must be for you."

Ben drew a deep breath and helped himself to a glass of water and nodded. Sanders had gentle eyes and a sincerity that seemed real. But his reputation was as a tough gritty lawyer with the kind of guts to take on Goliath if he had to.

"We'll get right to it, if you don't mind, Ben. I'm wondering … were you at all aware of what was to occur to you when you entered the building on that Saturday morning, or for that matter when you were in the headmaster's office prior to so called disciplinary action being taken?" Sanders enquired.

"Not at all," answered Ben, tensely.

Sanders scribbled something and the paralegal typed away on her recording device.

"From the time you arrived at school that Saturday, can you go over the events with us?" Sanders hesitated and continued. "And I repeat, Ben, I know this is difficult, but you may have to go over it several times, until we are perfectly clear on this."

Ben described in detail the dark hallways, the echo of his footfalls against the cold stone floors, and his knock on the headmaster's door. After a moment's delay as he sipped from the water glass, Ben then described the incredible indignity he felt as he was ordered to strip naked. He then briefly and tersely recounted the sodomy. Even now, so many years later, the shock was real. The pall over his spirit was overwhelming.

The three others present all looked on without saying a word for a full minute or two. Eventually, O'Donnell broke the ice.

"Are you up for more questions?" The taller, broader lawyer asked looking into Ben's eyes. Ben thought he saw them glistening, but wasn't sure.

"Yeah, I am OK" said Ben, breathing rapidly and visibly shaken, but mustering a weak smile. Always considerate of others, he followed with: "Thanks, I am sure this is tough for you guys too.

Chapter 10
Justice Beckons

When Ben completed recounting his experience, the two attorneys looked at each other.

"Ben will you excuse us for a moment? Marla, can you escort Ben to the waiting room please?"

Ben followed the secretary into the waiting room and sat on the edge of his seat, unconsciously tapping his foot as if rhythmically keeping tempo on the pedal of a drum. He wondered what the two lawyers were discussing, whether they were trying to figure out a way to let him down easy. Fuck! He had read all about Sanders' previous victories, his go-for-the-jugular success in nailing these bastards, and he couldn't imagine the attorneys refusing this challenge. On the other hand, his partner may not be so keen...

"Maybe they're hung up on my inability to pay," he thought and the second-guessing continued a full 10 minutes before they called him back into the room.

"Sorry about that," Sanders said. "We're a partnership and when the stakes are this high, we have to be sure we are both comfortable in taking on such a case."

"Of course," Ben said, nodding.

"This is serious. As we see it, your former headmaster, James A. Mayron, has just been elected Pope Alexander IX. The Vatican notoriously does not respond to complaints but this alleged incident violated both criminal and civil law. It is highly unusual, given the perpetrator's position." Sanders paused and took a sip of water before continuing. "Criminal charges will be difficult to pursue because Vatican City was granted sovereignty in 1929 and as such is virtually above the law, kind of like a diplomat committing a crime here in the states and getting off scot free, you see?"

Ben nodded and Sanders continued.

"Still, there are things that we can do from here in America," Sanders said, sitting on the edge of the table, hands outstretched. "First, we can contact St. Adolphus High School and see if we can negotiate a settlement with them. It will be up to them, since the statute of limitations has run out, but I'm confident they will want to keep this from going public."

"Now, Vatican sovereignty aside, Mayron is still alive and well. However, while the Vatican enjoys its diplomatic immunity, we have considerable leverage against the Church by threatening to go public with your allegations. We can and will use the press and will conduct investigations to see if there were others who were assaulted by Mayron."

With this, Sanders got up, and stood in front of Ben. Ben stood too, realizing his meeting had come to an end. He also realized that both attorneys were now fully on board with him, and he smiled inwardly at the thought.

"Attorney O'Donnell and I will formulate a strategy after researching the case law and get back to you in a few days,"

Sanders said, shaking Ben's hand. "You are sober and that's a good thing. You'll need your wits about you. I'm not going to lie to you, Ben. This will be tough. Try not to discuss this matter at all with anyone outside your inner circle and just keep it all together. Thank you so much for your courage in coming forward and sharing this with us."

Ben nodded and put on his coat to leave. "I am willing to do whatever it takes to recover from this," he said, glancing backward to the three people still in the room. A tear formed in his eye and he turned to leave but stopped and said, "Attorney Sanders, Attorney O'Donnell, I appreciate *your* courage as well!" None of the three men could predict how this would all play out, but they each recognized it would be an intense, hard-fought battle.

Ben showed himself to the exit and slowly walked back to his car. He felt relieved and somehow unburdened, but he noticed a growing feeling of pressure too. He got in his car, adjusted his mirror, put the keys in and steeled himself for the ride through the Manhattan business day traffic. He saved his real thoughts until he hit I-84 heading into Connecticut.

As he drove, he arrived at a conclusion: the disgraceful assault perpetrated on him by the new Pope had hampered his entire life. It had robbed him of his potential, his happiness, his dignity. That ended here and now, he decided. By seeking counsel and representation as well as pushing himself on his own, he was drawing a line in the metaphoric sand and taking back what had been stolen from him.

He was now more determined than ever to claim justice, even if it meant upturning his life to do so. The rest of the drive north centered around those thoughts and before he knew it, he was only a few miles from his apartment. He parked his car on a side street and rode the elevator up to his floor.

As he entered his apartment, he took off his coat, hanging it neatly in the closet. He then sat down in his favorite chair and rubbed his temples, still deep in thought. He went over the events of the afternoon and then showered and fixed dinner. While his dinner was simmering, he grabbed his guitar and went out onto the porch where he sang with it, alone and silent, his tall frame silhouetted by stars and a sliver of a moon.

After dinner, he called Jamie, filling her in on the meeting. After a brief pause, he asked her to dinner the following day. She said yes and, after hanging up, Ben turned on the computer and set about working on his manuscript. When he finally quit for the day, he had written another 10 more pages and was progressing well. His book was coming along nicely, and so was he.

After shutting down the computer, Ben dimmed the lights and sat quietly in the semi-darkness, reviewing the day's events and making plans for the next day. He used this type of meditation or reflection for the past several years in addition to his regular Buddhist meditation. It was all about the reflected life. Besides he knew that if ever he needed to be clear-minded, that time was right now. Thursday morning he awoke early, filled with energy and eager to hit the ground running for another productive day. He was to call attorney Sanders on Friday for an update, but in the meantime he would not waste any time. Errands and chores done and several more pages written, Ben cleaned up and headed out to see Jamie. He still loved her very much and genuinely enjoyed her company. In fact, after the divorce, they became better friends than ever and usually spoke every day and saw each other three or more times each week.

It was raining when Ben picked her up and in a way, it matched his mood. She got in the passengers side and they drove to their favorite restaurant, speaking very little. Jamie sensed Ben's unease; she, too, was aware of the stakes that he faced. They ate quietly, chatting only a little, avoiding the giant elephant in the room, Ben's meeting with Sanders. Loosened up over coffee and desert, Ben finally did tell her about his meeting the day before and that it had gone well.

"I am sure the attorney will handle it correctly," Jamie said with her concerned wisdom intact. Clearly they would one day have to have a more in-depth discussion about the assault – she only knew there had been "an incident" – but Ben wasn't ready to divulge the details to her yet. Ben dropped her off, saying goodnight without any physical contact or romantic advances.

When he got back to his place, Ben called Barb, filling her in on the events of the last two days. As always, Barb made sure he was alright, offered her support, and said they would meet in a few days at the next RAVOC meeting. He sent an e-mail to Kelly and Carl too, letting them know he was doing ok and that he'd fill them in on his meeting with the attorney in the next few days. He also sent one to Paul Adams, updating him on the meeting as well. He would have done it yesterday but wanted to process it so he understood where things were, before sharing it with them all. That night, he went to bed, cold, lonely, and wondering where this journey was taking him.

On that mid-April morning, Ben called Attorney Sanders as agreed upon at 10 a.m. Alicia, the secretary answered and put him on hold briefly. The attorney was tied up but she said he would get back to him in the afternoon. Ben was keenly aware that this whole process was going to take time and he was determined to be patient.

When Sanders did call, his tone was cheerful. After dispensing with small talk, he began his assessment of the case.

"I am deeply sorry that this happened to you and we will see what we can do to make it right. We may never be successful, given the resources and power the Vatican wields, but we will indeed try." He continued, "Let me get to right the point. We have several options here. One, we can sue the Vatican and St. Adolphus High School separately or simultaneously to gain restitution. Chances are that St. Adolphus will offer a settlement fairly quickly and the Vatican will most likely work discretely through the school."

"There's a wrench thrown into the typical equation once it becomes known that the perpetrator in this case is the Pope. That puts a whole new slant on things. We really don't know which way it will go. What we have in our corner however is the power of the press, and believe me, the Church is not going to want that force unleashed. The problem is, we don't want you to suffer any further, and these guys will stop at nothing to keep their power. They will break you if they have to, figuratively and perhaps even physically."

"I see," was all Ben could say in response.

"I suggest we go the two-fold route of filing openly with the Vatican and your former High School at the same time, and search in the meantime for others who were sexually assaulted by this man. How do you feel about that?" Sanders asked Ben.

Ben said "That sounds like a strong plan, sir. I want the truth told and appreciate your going to bat for me. I realize it will mean a significant investment of time and resources on your part, and of course, I will cooperate to the full extent of my abilities. I believe that goes for RAVOC as well. Fill me in on what I – and RAVOC -- should do".

The attorney then recommended that Ben lay low for the time being. "And if things get heated, just do your best to keep it together. That will be crucial for the integrity of this case. I cannot stress it enough, Ben, stay out of trouble and maintain your dignity."

Ben promised he would and they agreed to talk again on the following Tuesday as a follow up. He said goodbye and held the receiver in his hands a few moments after the call had been disconnected. After he put the phone down, he paced back and forth across the room for a few minutes thinking deeply about the events that were about to occur. By now, it was mid-afternoon. He stared out the window of his apartment. It was still rainy and gloomy. He knew there would be significant attention focused in his direction in the near future, but he also knew that this was much bigger than him and he was prepared to accept whatever came down the pike for that reason.

Ben was no hero, but he refused to push what happened to him under the rug any longer, nor did he intend to remain a victim. Besides, perhaps there were other victims that hadn't yet come to terms with their abuse and maybe, just maybe, his taking action would help clear the path for them, by giving them the courage to stand up and name their abusers. For this to be successful, though, Ben needed to clear his heart and mind and summon a steely resolve from every fiber of his being.

PART THREE

Retribution

Chapter 11
Retribution

Ben paid a visit to his son Brad on Saturday and the two grabbed lunch together. He loved the 25-year-old and had a deep respect for his warm, intelligent manner and his insightful humor. Having gone through what he did, the first prerogative for him towards his son was that he would always protect him, which he absolutely did, like a bear protecting his cub. Money was always tight, so they did not have as much enjoyment as other kids and he wished he could have given Brad more – the stylish $100 sneakers all the other kids supposedly had, the trip to Europe during High School, etc., etc., but he did do his best as a father, he acknowledged to himself on the drive home. Brad was raised with a healthy spirituality and good, sound honesty. Jamie was responsible for much of this. For all her faults, she was a strong, loving mother.

In two weeks time, Ben's manuscript had grown to more than 150 pages and he was on track to complete it in the next few weeks. After writing most of the weekend, he took a break Monday night and sat in silence a while longer than normal in anticipation of Tuesday's phone conference. When Sanders called, after dispensing with pleasantries, he got right to the point.

"Here's where we stand, Ben," Sanders started. "We've gathered the information we need in order to proceed. I suggest strongly that we approach St. Adolphus and make the case that coming to a settlement would be in their best interest, and see what they say."

"Sounds good," Ben said during a pause.

"They will of course notify the Vatican and that's when all hell could break loose," Sanders continued. "With this kind of behavior in his background, Mayron should never have accepted the Papacy, but that's not our fault, nor is it our fight. Once the Vatican gets wind of this, they probably will want to settle the matter quickly and quietly in order to preserve their secrets. In other words, they'll throw money at this case and will want nothing more than for this to go away."

"We are not going to name you initially, nor will they know who we are making the claim on behalf of just yet. That information we will hold until their reply comes through." The attorney spoke cautiously. "We work closely with a contact here in the Northeast, a former priest who was himself abused in the seminary. He is excellent at uncovering other victims and survivors. He's already on the case, making discreet inquiries and utilizing various means in order to find others who may have been molested by Mayron. We need to take our time and do this right. Give us a week or so and we will confer again on, say, next Thursday or Friday, OK?" the attorney said.

"What then?" asked Ben.

"Well, as I said earlier, they may offer to settle, but then again, we may have to commence litigation against the Vatican itself. They have massive resources and may well drag things out and more, drag you through the mud, so you need to be prepared for some very close scrutiny of your background."

"Right," Ben said.

"And that reminds me – is there anything else in your past that we need to be aware of, Ben?" Attorney Sanders asked. "I need to know exactly where we stand and don't want any surprises turning up in their enquiries. Aside from what you have told us already, are there any deep dark secrets that you haven't shared before? It is common for abuse victims to act out and replay the -- "

"Sir, there's nothing, I assure you," Ben broke in. "Other than the arrest for possession of a controlled substance over 30 years ago, there's nothing else."

"Good then. Regardless, we have to wait for a reply from St. Adolphus and our priest collaborator before proceeding, you understand? We'll speak again next week. If anything comes up I or someone here in the firm will certainly call you, and you, please, do the same," Sanders said, ending the phone conference.

Ben had his affidavit ready along with his transcripts from High School that Paul Adams advised him to obtain, and at this point he was a bundle of raw nerves. He was uncertain what to do if St. Adolphus offered him a settlement. In his heart he wanted to take his case all the way to Rome, but the question was, could he stand what they may throw at him?

For someone who had been through so much, including living as a bi-polar and recovering alcoholic, he observed and internalized a great deal. Though he didn't drive a fancy car, belong to the local golf club or have a million dollar home, he was no slouch. He carried himself well and was quite content with the direction his life was taking at this point. Perhaps his greatest failing was that he was so honest, Ben thought to himself. This made him appear almost naïve in a very cunning world, but because he was inwardly aware of that reality, such knowledge gave him a power over many who otherwise would have looked down upon him.

Ben knew that the Church had taken some huge hits in the last few decades and had shown itself to be extremely vulnerable. His ultimate goal in writing and releasing his book was to call it out and shine a spotlight on all the myriad crimes it had committed over the centuries. RAVOC was only 24 years old but had become a driving force in holding the Church accountable for its nefarious and criminal activities. And of course, he detailed all of RAVOC's allegations and battles against the church in his book. But RAVOC had focused primarily on the heinous aspect of sex crimes alone, not on some of the other dark dealings of the Vatican, which were considered criminal activities on the International front and which he bravely included.

He covered in his book the history of the Vatican and its founding nearly 1700 years ago, when it was considered the cornerstone of all Christianity. He also went back further, based on Joseph Campbell's work on mythology and others as well, and included notable parallels between Jesus and Horus of Egypt, born 1,000 years before Jesus Christ on December 25th of a Virgin Birth. Like Jesus, his birth was visited by three Kings and he, too, began his public ministry at age 30, had 12 disciples, was crucified, died and was buried. He, too, was raised from the tomb three days later. Horus was also called the son of God and the Lamb of God as well. Other coincidences (he used that term loosely), that he included were the fact that most of Moses' story was borrowed from other sources and that the Christian springtime holiday "Easter" came from the Babylonian "Ishtar" the goddess of fertility and war.

In the course of Ben's studies, he found little in the Christian Myth – that's what he came to view it as -- that was truthful or real. Jesus Himself was not declared a God until the reign of Constantine in the 4th Century, when Christianity became the national religion as a convenient tool to control the empire. The majority of writings from the gospels, he discovered, were not at all factual. He knew his book would rock the U.S. mainstream at least, and that he was opening himself up to serious criticism, scrutiny and millions of naysayers. But his argument was a simple one: How are we to believe what was written decades, and in some instances centuries after Christ's purported crucifixion and believe it, and the events surrounding it, as real? We have enormous difficulty in scribing events that occurred a mere few years ago with accuracy, such as the genesis of the war in Vietnam. And yet, we believe blindly.

After researching and writing about the history of Christianity, Ben went into the specifics of the Catholic Church for which he understandably had very little love. He included in his book several photographs of Adolph Hitler exiting various Catholic Churches as Cardinals and Bishops raised their hands in salute to the dictactor. Hitler repeatedly affirmed that he was a Catholic and always would be a Catholic, and in the 1920s, the Papal Nuncio who was later to become Pope Pius XII, helped the Fuhrer establish his power base in Germany while padding his own coffers mightily. The fact is, the only Nazi criminal excommunicated after the war was Goebbels, and his sin was not the assault and massacre of millions of Jews. Instead, he was excommunicated for marrying a Protestant! Hitler was never called to account by the church for the grave acts he carried out, and it was as though they turned a blind eye to his crimes altogether!

"There has never been anything more grandiose on the face of the earth than the hierarchical organization of the Catholic Church," Nazi Germany's dark prince, Hitler, said at one official function. "I transferred much of this organization into my own party."

In reading all of this while researching for his book, Ben was disgusted to see this nexus of state and religion, and even more so, knowing Hitler's history of genocide and depraved, murderous indifference. While Hitler was operating on a grand scale wreaking havoc across all of Europe, the Slavic Region's predominantly Catholic Croatians were so brutal to the Serbs that the Serbs actually petitioned the Gestapo and Nazi SS for intercession, but to no avail. As a result, hundreds of thousands of non-Catholics were forced to renounce their religion or face death.

Ben went back even further in his book to the Crusades and the Time of the Inquisitions, an era that spanned a much larger portion of history than one would suppose, from the 1100's to the 1800's. The Congregation for the Doctrine of the Christian Faith (CDF) continues to operate within the Church to this day as the last remaining arm of that dark wing of the so-called Holy Roman Empire. Predating the Nazis by many centuries, this body of the Vatican singled out Jews and others considered heretics, and tortured, imprisoned in ghettoes, and even killed them en masse in the name of the Church Their actions were especially brutal towards women. In addition, the Spanish and Portuguese Conquistadors who acted as servants of the Papacy raped, pillaged, and plundered indigenous peoples, from Asia to the Native Americans in North America. Church Missions were established as forts within eyeshot of one another so that these territories could be captured and established first for the Pope and then for the Crown, in that order.

Ben summarized what he'd learned in his as-yet untitled book: the Catholic Church sanctioned and even perpetuated the genocide of Muslims, Jews and other non-Christians for centuries and got away with it. He was stunned that such a murderous and bloody power as that wielded by the Church could have gone unchecked for so long. After detailing so much darkness in the form of genocide and acts of physical violence, Ben felt it necessary to include the sordid history of monetary corruption and abuse of power that was rampant in the Catholic Church throughout its history up to recent years. The FBI and Interpol were even recently investigating links between the Vatican, the Mafia, and the Russian Mob with regard to expanding the heroin trade in Eastern Europe.

Pope John Paul I was set to acknowledge and accept responsibility for much of the Church's dark history just a few weeks after taking office in the hopes of starting a new, brighter chapter. Ben mentioned this in his book and noted allegations by the FBI that John Paul I was believed to have been silenced before he could do so, allegedly by assassination. The theory was that digitalis was slipped in among his medicines, purportedly by his own doctor and that he succumbed quickly in the Papal Chambers.

The past transgressions somehow managed to fly under the radar of most of the Church's faithful. It was the revelations of the recent decades' predatory sex scandals and cover-ups by Bishops and even the Vatican that had Catholics everywhere reconsidering their loyalty. Letters from the Vatican to local church officials were unearthed that became one more smoking gun, according to global news sources. The documents were written to officials in two different countries ordering the local prelates not to cooperate with law enforcement officials under any circumstances, basically affirming that the Church considers itself above the law, including in matters of clergy sexual abuse. Without a courageous Pope like John Paul I who had been prepared to shed light on the flaws and remedy them, Ben wrote in his book's conclusion, there was little hope for the Vatican as a sacred institution.

Chapter 12
Taking Action

The following Wednesday night Ben attended a RAVOC meeting in a small tucked away conference room at the local hospital. Closed to all except survivors of sexual abuse from priests and other clergy, these meetings were a great comfort to Ben and the other attendees. Barb was there as always, moderating the meeting and leading the discussion. The discussions were actually one-sided as each person told his or her own story, at times relating the steps they were taking to heal while the others listened attentively. At other times the speaker would relate the difficulty of dealing with life emotionally and facing up to his or her predator(s). Most, like Ben left their childhood churches behind never to look back. Some remained members of the Catholic Church, but Barb told Ben confidentially after one meeting that those who remained in the Church were far less successful in coming to grips with the extent of their damage.

In the meetings, there was a kind of unconditional love and acceptance shown toward each new member and judgment was never passed. Members come to believe that a person would have a better grasp on their own journey as they listened to how other members dealt with personal abuse. In short, it was a collective healing group based on every individual's needs, rights and responsibilities as each saw fit. Some would stay for just one meeting; others were old timers, who'd been members for years. Some became active in the inner-workings of RAVOC and worked to promote its agenda which always centered around healing and justice.

At that night's meeting, late in May, Ben finally opened up about who his perpetrator was. It came as no surprise to Barb, who already knew, but Gene and the others had no idea and they were all dumbfounded and listened in rapt silence as Ben filled them all in on the progress he had made and on what steps were about to be taken. Gene had a background in police work and was very sharp in his observations. When Ben had finished speaking, Gene asked a couple of simple questions to clarify things, then weighed his words carefully and spoke from the heart.

"Ben, I didn't know, I am so sorry for you. I see now why you chose not to speak out much at all." Gene was careful not to offer direct advice, in accordance with RAVOC's unwritten code. There were times, however, when all of RAVOC's members would be called to action and this was one of them. The long-time member offered some observations and recommended several steps, some of which Ben had already taken. He also offered his assistance in research and whatever else Ben might require. The remainder of the meeting was lively and discussion surrounded the topic of the Church's code of secrecy and its practice of moving predatory priests from parish to parish to conceal the criminal issues it was so lax in dealing with. When the meeting adjourned, Gene pulled Ben aside.

"Here's my phone number, Ben. Don't hesitate to call me any time – night or day. This is one tough road you have ahead of you and I want you to know I am here for you," Gene said, giving Ben a hug after handing him a sheet of paper with his number and address on it.

"Thanks so much, Gene, you have no idea how much that means to me," Ben said, taking his information gratefully. "I may call on you sooner than you think!"

Ben left, unaware that Gene and Barb and the other directors of the Central Connecticut group stayed late after the meeting to talk about his unfolding situation and the likely attention it would bring to the organization's local chapter. The board agreed Barbara should play point person and consult with the leaders in Chicago as often as necessary. She would keep them abreast of any new developments in Ben's case as they all agreed that something very important was about to occur and that it was best to be on the alert.

After the first semi-public disclosure of the identity of his assailant, Ben went home alone, grabbed his guitar and went out to play quietly on the porch. After some time, he set the guitar down and, inhaling the early spring air, began to weep. He sank down onto the porch and stayed there for some time, expelling the demons of his past. He felt alone, uncertain, drained.

He had gotten used to sleeping fitfully over the last several weeks, anxious and alert to strange sounds. When he finally fell asleep, it was 1:45 a.m. and he was exhausted. The next afternoon, he received a call from Brenda. She was simply checking up on him and reminded him that he had the full support of RAVOC. Ben filled her in on Sanders' strategy and they agreed that it was best to wait on a response from his former high school. As so many others in RAVOC had, she told Ben that she was available anytime for him to call including at 3 a.m. if necessary.

After hanging up the phone, Brenda reflected for a while. She had co-founded RAVOC for a reason and while she was acutely sensitive to the needs of survivors, she also believed the Roman Catholic Church was the biggest hoax ever perpetrated on the face of the earth and that it had bred a toxic culture of predators that destroyed the lives of hundreds of thousands of young people. She was tenacious, and, along with Dan and others had learned how to use the press to force these bastards, as she considered them, to comply. It wasn't easy since all the bishops they encountered fell back on their code of secrecy and used the church's sovereignty to evade responsibility. She and many others within RAVOC believed the church's coffers were filled with the tithes of the still unsuspecting masses who blindly trusted them for their spiritual well-being when in fact these bishops, cardinals, popes and priests were actually spiritually bankrupt themselves. She hated them and steeped herself in these emotions for a time tonight.

Brenda thought about the ironic situation RAVOC found itself in now. The organization was not new to charging the Vatican's highest office with misdeeds. RAVOC actually dealt with the former Pope, Boniface, when the fledgling non-profit sued on behalf of a deaf man whose life had been destroyed when he was a child by a pedophile priest in Wisconsin. It was RAVOC's first case, in fact, and during discovery, they learned the priest had molested more than 200 children in a similar manner.

The former Pope, then Cardinal von Reichsinger, knew about the situation but took no action to remove the priest or to alleviate the suffering of the youths involved, thus making him complicit in the heinous crime. RAVOC made the case that since von Reichsinger was the head of the CDF, it was his duty to discipline wayward priests that came to his attention. In this particular case, von Reichsinger was alerted numerous times about the egregious actions of this one priest and chose to ignore the problem. Instead, because the offending priest was in his later years by the time the allegations were made, the Cardinal kept the priest in his position, hoping the matter would fade quietly from the public eye. Some 200 youths' lives were ruined by that one priest!

To Brenda it seems the greatest calling of the Pope – at least most modern day Popes -- was to protect the enormous wealth of the Vatican and maintain its Sovereignty so that it could remain untouchable by international law. Sadly, hundreds of similar cases surfaced since Brenda started RAVOC, all pointing to the sharp refusal of the Vatican to work within the law and to a gross disregard for the sufferings of others in its care.

People in developed countries were beginning to see through this horrific façade and were leaving the Church by the tens of thousands, Brenda knew. But those living in underdeveloped countries still clung to the exploitive mysticism of the Church and found a measure of comfort in it, and yet rarely were their lives changed for the better. "Opiate for the masses," Karl Marx had said. Brenda and many others in RAVOC were inclined to agree.

On Friday, Ben was on tenderhooks as he awaited a call from Sanders. The attorney had fired the first shot across the bow of the good ship Vatican and Ben was very anxious to hear what the response would be. He checked in with Paul Adams and Carl and went about his day oblivious to the other people in his building as things started to progress in his case. That afternoon, Sanders finally called.

"Ben, I spoke with the head of the Jesuit Order in New York, Greg Camacho, who is in charge of St. Adolphus High School and the entire New York City Jesuit Order," Sanders said.

"Okay," Ben said.

"He has been made aware of our claim and has asked for two weeks to reply to us. I am arranging the paperwork to be sent to him as we speak. I haven't told him what we want, and that can wait until we are further along."

"Of course," Ben said as the attorney broke for a breath.

"At this point, they have your name, Ben and more than likely, they will want to do some investigating and are probably doing so even now, given the gravity of the situation."

"Oh. Sure…" Ben said.

"What I'd like you to do is simply go about your business and wait for my next call. Are you OK with that?" Sanders asked.

"Of course…" Ben said. "I don't have much choice, do I? I'll be fine, don't worry…"

After hanging up, Ben called Paul Adams to let him know the papers were being served.

"They have my name now," Ben said, alarm ebbing into his voice.

"It'll be fine, Ben. Don't you worry. I'm working on an idea and would like to meet with you again soon if you can make it into the city?"

"Sure, Paul. Next week?" Ben suggested.

"Thursday works. Can you do Thursday?" Paul asked, consulting his calendar.

"Yes, absolutely… say midday?" Ben asked.

"Perfect. Let's meet at that midtown café again, okay?" Paul said.

"Great, see you there, Thursday at noon." Ben said and hung up, feeling somewhat relieved. He had confidence in the savvy Paul and was glad he was on his side. Though he placed his trust in Sanders too, he knew the attorney had to approach his case from a business / legal perspective. By contrast, Paul was looking out for his integrity. He knew that Ben was squeamish about taking a settlement, thinking it was selling out, and also thinking of alternatives.

Ben then called Jamie to fill her in and invite her to dinner on the following night. He also updated Kelly, Carl and Brenda to let them know the proverbial Pandora's Box had been opened. Each offered their support. Kelly was ready at the keyboard to help with backup research if necessary, Carl suggested Ben come down and visit soon, and Brenda said RAVOC was prepared to do whatever was required to help Ben and Sanders as well.

After the calls, Ben went through the rest of the day cheerfully on the exterior, but while running errands, a growing sense of unease took over. The manuscript was taking shape and he was now reviewing the draft, more than halfway done. Needing office supplies, he headed to town and turned the car into the office supply superstore parking lot, noticing a car behind him do the same at the last minute.

"They are probably investigating me right now," he thought to himself. "Probably even tailing me at this very moment." He put the paranoia out of his mind and focused his thoughts on the manuscript and dinner the next night with Jamie.

When he picked her up the following evening, he brought Jamie up to date on his case. Several times he reached for her hand because in his heart he still very much wanted her in his life. She avoided his grasp, though, and without saying anything, sent a message that he would have to accept their present reality for now. Realizing this, Ben refused to close the door on their relationship for good, hoping someday they would find their way back to one another, perhaps even grow old together.

When he went home, Ben once again picked up pen and paper and continued his editing the book that was intended as a powerful portrayal of the sexual and moral corruption that had gripped the Roman Catholic world. Truly this was a crumbling empire, he thought, noting that every day the news carried headlines unearthing decades-old scandals and new fresh ones as well. In reality, the scandalous news hit the Church at all levels. It was no longer just the predatory pedophilic priests, but also extortion, corruption, money laundering, and even murder! Was it the denial of sexual fulfillment or forced celibacy that had created this, or was it merely that the tenets of the Church are a huge hoax not supported by anything remotely disguised as reality? Ben wondered. He suspected he knew the answers. But he also knew that freedom of religion was one of the most powerful and respected rights of our country and most other countries within the international community as well.

He left his writing and sank into his comfortable lounge chair reflecting that his own philosophy was to 'live and let live', or, 'to each his own'. He also knew the dangers of not speaking out, though and now he was acutely aware that he was caught in a real Catch 22 situation. To speak out may blackball him in many circles. It may even cost him his life, since his case pointed right to the top of the Vatican, one of the most powerful bodies in the world. But he also realized what it would cost him not to speak out, and chose the former as the only possible path that he could rightfully embark on. He remembered what Edmund Burke, the historian, had once said and he said it out loud to himself: "All that is necessary for the triumph of evil is for good men to do nothing."

Ben knew he was a good man, and it was inconceivable at this stage for him to do nothing. In addition, he was at a turning point in his life, throwing off the cloak of victimhood and moving swiftly from powerlessness to becoming fully empowered and free. He no longer felt guilty or in any way diminished as a person because of the assault and the resultant failures it set up in his life. Finally freed from those shackles, he realized they were perpetrated on him without his consent and now was his time to fulfill his potential and do what he believed he was destined to do.

Ben realized as he sat at his desk holding the manuscript that this was perhaps why he was born. It was his karma to not only experience the misery, the assault and the pain, but later to learn from it, rise above it, and share with others what he had learned. If it meant a reckoning for the Church as well, then so be it!

Chapter 13
The Real Intelligence

The following Thursday morning, a call came through from Attorney Sanders' office. Ben eagerly picked up the phone and answered. It was the secretary, Alicia, who addressed him first, but the attorney came on a moment later.

"Ben, we have some interesting news. Representatives for St. Adolphus have worked through the information we provided and want to meet with us. A date hasn't been set as of yet, but they have asked us to keep this quiet, something we are not obliged to do, but which we will if you have no objections. Are you willing to go to Jesuit headquarters in New York City sometime in the next few weeks?" He gave Ben time to think.

Ben said he would feel more comfortable meeting at Sander's New York office. His attorney agreed and said that he would get back to Ben regarding the date, time and place of the meeting. After a brief pause and reflecting on his client's circumstances, Sanders asked Ben if he was OK with this planned meeting. Ben thanked him for considering his predicament and said that he could handle it, expressing hope that the process would not drag on forever.

After the call, Ben went back to editing his novel, based on some new feedback from Kelly. To call it a novel was a stretch as it mirrored his own life to an uncanny degree, he decided, but it was safer to market this as a work of fiction and change some of the elements and names. Paul Adams had been a great help in framing the book that way. And with Kelly's sharp editorial eye, well, Ben was confident the book would be marketable in the not so distant future.

One of RAVOC's top three contacts, Brenda, Barb and Gene, reached out to Ben daily to ensure he was working through the minefields he was forced to deal with and check up on his emotional soundness. The daily calls also fed him news and served to obtain updates from Ben in return, regarding his case. It was clear to Ben and the others that there was a strong likelihood that any settlement on his case would include a clause prohibiting him from speaking out about the rape, which was contrary to their goals. If that happened, RAVOC would be forced to keep this case silent too. What then of true justice? Would it be silenced as well?

In the meantime, more instances of clergy abuse were revealed in the news every day, it seemed, reaching across the ocean to Ireland, France and Germany as well as to Belgium and Australia. Attention was growing like an avalanche cascading down upon the Vatican from every direction. For instance, in Brussels, RAVOC, in its first international effort, brought a case to the police and the media simultaneously. In this case, the police took swift action against the Archbishop who had allegedly covered up for one of his subordinates, a Bishop who had repeatedly abused minors throughout his earlier career as a parish priest. In that case, the police had even gone into a previous Archbishop's tomb to search out and dig up records of abuse that had reportedly been hidden there. It seemed to Ben that law enforcement authorities were finally engaged now, in contrast to earlier times when the secrecy of the Church's hierarchy had reigned supreme.

Ben discovered the news was breaking not just about clergy abuse, but money laundering as well. There were even reports of a male prostitution ring being uncovered by the Italian Police in Vatican City that pointed uncomfortably close to the Vatican and former Pope, Boniface. That scandal surfaced when a police investigation into corruption at the Vatican turned up an organized male prostitution network linked to one of Boniface's senior aides and a Vatican chorister. Both were speedily removed from their positions. Something was rotten in the state of the Vatican and finally, eyes were indeed opening.

"The allegations were made public when Italian newspapers published transcripts of phone calls recorded by the police," a British news outlet reported in an online article. "Police had been conducting an unrelated corruption investigation at the time. Apparently the tapes record Angelo Baldini, a representative of His Holiness negotiating with Thomas Hioom, a 26-year-old Ghanian Vatican Chorister, about men he wanted brought to him for sexual purposes."

Ben bookmarked and shared the online article with a few friends in his e-mail address book. Then he pushed back from the monitor and rested his head against the back of the chair. There was so much to take in! But armed with this and a myriad of other damning pieces of information, Ben was ready to take on the task which had been laid at his doorstep as a consequence of what happened so many years before. He was entirely ready. If it weren't for RAVOC and his circle of friends he might have just ignored it all, but even Jamie encouraged his efforts.

They met that weekend and went for a long walk in the cool spring air. Ben asked her if she would go with him to New York City, and without hestitating, she said of course. She too was beginning to feel part of this. After all, during their marriage she had been robbed of intimacy since Ben found it extremely hard to share that side of himself. Now that he had time to heal, Ben was becoming more comfortable with who he was. What's more, he had a newfound love of life and was far more open with people than he had ever been, she observed.

Ben explained as they discussed that very subject that this was a result of the journey he had embarked on for so many years. He told her that he had always believed in himself, but now he was being tested in ways he never could have foreseen. Interestingly enough, he was more confident than ever in the outcome.

"Maybe I'm just being idealistic," he said, shrugging.

She touched his hand and looked closely into his eyes.

"Not at all. You are very wise, Ben Clancy!" She let her hand linger on his that evening and he did not move it for a long time. And then, it was only to take the check offered by the waitress.

Ben stepped up his meditations over the next two weeks finding it kept him centered. He continued to work closely with Kelly on the editing process on his novel and updated Paul Adams as it neared completion. Paul advised that it was best to keep quiet about the book's contents until the time was right. He also said he was confident they would know the right time when it came...

Paul had mentioned a while back and reminded Ben about a plan he was formulating that might allow for Ben to consider a legal settlement while at the same time refuse the anticipated silence clause. He was researching legal precedent for the unconventional maneuver, he explained to Ben, and would advise him as time went on if it looked viable. Paul also updated Carl on his thoughts and Carl was highly supportive.

"If anyone can help you turn this to your advantage, its Paul," Carl said when he and Ben talked the next day.

"So what is he, a fixer?" Ben asked, mystified by Adams.

"Something like that," Carl answered. "Just follow his recommendations and you will do fine."

"What's his real story anyway?" Ben asked.

"Oh no, that's not for me to tell you," Carl interjected. "He'll explain it all when he's ready, I'm sure. Just hang in there with him, Ben."

"Okay Carl, I'm taking your word for it," Ben said.

The two brothers talked about the pro basketball standings and other news and hung up with Ben feeling more confident about Paul – and more appreciative of his brother as well.

Ben thought about Paul's warning to be wary and that his life might be in danger. For that reason, he let Brad know about the book and slowly educated him and Kelly on what his wishes were regarding publication of the manuscript and any financial gain that might come from either a settlement or sale of the manuscript, should anything happen to him. He let Jamie in on his wishes as well and let her know that if anything happened to him, there was a small insurance policy listing her as the beneficiary hidden in the bottom drawer of his desk. He was truly facing his own mortality and wanted to be prepared.

In the Vatican, there was a somber hush throughout the ancient hallways. Word had gotten to the recently elected Pope Alexander IX, previously known as Cardinal James A. Mayron, about the allegations overseas and he struggled fiercely to maintain his power through denial and secrecy. The Pontiff kept the truth even from his inner circle, including his Secretary of State, the second in command Cardinal Frenoso, who was originally from Buenos Aires. The Pope worried that his days might be numbered if the accuser spoke out. Unless drastic measures were taken that prevented this revelation, not only he, but the entire church could go down as well.

Though he had only been in office for a month, the new Pope took several weeks off, retreating to Castle Gandolfo, a country dwelling high up in the mountains of Northern Italy. Owned by the Vatican and historically used for Papal holidays, this retreat was hidden from the eyes of the world. Citing a health problem, but in reality to ponder his own defense, he rushed away to the expansive rural setting. When the call came through from Father Camacho at Jesuit Headquarters in New York, the Pope's secretary, Cardinal Ursine delivered the message with raised eyebrows. With not so subtle admonishment in his tone, Ursine recommended the Pope speak directly with the Vatican's Chief Counsel, the Prefect of the Apostolic Signatura, Cardinal Bergston.

"In such cases, of course, you must consult with him," Ursine said archly. "I will arrange a meeting for tomorrow here at Gandolfo, your Holiness."

Ursine turned and left before the Pope could protest.

At that meeting, the Pope maintained his innocence, denying the accusation and insisting that Mother Church stands above all such allegations.

"I will convey your response, your Excellency," Bergston replied.

The Pope continued lying to his own people, arrogantly believing he could manipulate the situation from a safe distance. After all, wasn't he the head of the CDF before becoming the Pope? He knew the ins and outs of the Vatican's power structure and how the game was played. Moreover, he knew where the skeletons were buried, and would use that information as leverage if he had to!

After receiving word from the Vatican's Chief Council about the Pope's blunt denial, Father Camacho called Attorney Sanders and was put through immediately.

"The Pope vehemently denies these allegations and we ask that there be no further discussion of the matter from here on in," Camacho told Sanders.

After a slight pause, Sanders weighed his words, cleared his throat and spoke.

"The Church might want to reconsider their stance as two more alleged victims have come forward who make similar claims that the new Pope molested them as well," the astute Sanders responded. "And this is just from his tenure at St. Adolphus."

Without needing to say it, Sanders knew Camacho would realize the press would be all over this if these multiple allegations were made public. "I'll give you 48 hours to change your thinking on this," Sanders continued in a gentle but persuasive tone.

Camacho agreed and asked for more time to share this new information with the Vatican.

"I'm sorry, but you understand my client is eager to resolve this case. I'll give you 72 hours," Sanders said and paused once again before going on.

"I don't envy you," Sanders said, acknowledging that Camacho was simply a go-between and in a difficult position. Ben's attorney had thought how he'd approach this conversation as soon as he learned of the additional victims. He could have taken a more direct, offensive attack but decided it would serve Ben's interests better to establish a rapport he hoped would increase his success during negotiations which he knew would be forthcoming. There was no way the Vatican would be able to ignore this since it was not just one allegation any longer.

After they hung up, Sanders immediately called Ben and filled him in on the conversation. He advised Ben to be patient, but to expect a settlement offer fairly quickly. Later that afternoon, Ben drove down Highway 9 to Old Saybrook, a place he went when he wanted to sort things out within himself.

As he walked along the beach he reflected on the implications of a settlement. Money would mean security, not just for himself, but also, for Jamie and Brad. It would also mean his life would gain credibility and though he wasn't a materially oriented person, would mean some lifelong dreams fulfilled, such as land, a place to create, and a pleasant future. It sounded wonderful, he thought. But as he stepped amid the seashells and driftwood gathered there, other thoughts weighed on him. As a former Catholic, he had a well-developed conscience and knew that no matter what the offer, he could never sell out the other victims if it meant accepting the silence clause. And he personally needed more than just money …

He needed acknowledgement from the Pope that his former Headmaster had fucked up Ben's life to an unbearable degree. He needed to know that the twisted pedophile would be cast out from the Papacy and treated as a pariah for his conduct. And he needed assurances that the Church would no longer harbor, cover up for, or condone – even in secret – this type of abuse and evil.

Two weeks went by without an answer from the Jesuits. Ben filled the time by working with Kelly to fine tune the manuscript with feedback and recommendations from Carl and Paul who had both started reading it. After studying it in depth, Paul said Ben's book threatened the Vatican in a way that very few other documents had in many years.

"This comes at a time when the Roman Catholic Church is already vulnerable in light of the many scandals that have been made public," Paul observed, drawing Ben into a discussion about the alleged Vatican plots to bring harm to and actually murder those who spoke ill of the Church, as well as the nexus between the Church and the U.S. Mafia to expand the church's underworld reach.

"You know, living in Connecticut, I sit in one of the main arteries of the Mafia," Ben said over the telephone.

"I realize this," Paul said. "That's why I urge you to keep this under wraps for now. We'll know when the time is right to move forward with publication and press coverage.

Still, Ben felt very vulnerable and thought using an assumed name in publishing of the work would be in his best interest.

"Let's see how things play out," Paul advised and they agreed Paul would call Ben again in a few days time.

During the day, Ben was his usual cheerful self, enjoying the spring foliage, greeting neighbors warmly, and going about his business. But at night, his anxiety grew. He wasn't afraid per se. He knew the stakes of what he was dealing with and he knew ultimately that it would be worth the cost. While he absolutely did not want it to happen, he was prepared to give his life to expose the truth if it came to that.

Chapter 14
And So it Begins

When the manuscript was finished and to his liking, Ben made several digital and hard copies which he stored in various safe places. He gave one copy of each to Brad, with specific instructions should anything happen to him. Brad assured Ben that he would do whatever was necessary to get the work published when the time came, though he was sure no harm would befall his dad. Brad was proud of his father, despite his quirks, and saw him with new eyes after Ben moved into his own place and confronted his childhood demons. He had very little in the way of luxuries, but Brad had been raised to be content without trappings and found most Americans' penchant for buying the newest, latest and greatest toys absurd at best, and was thankful for his father's example in that.

The two had dinner together and discussed numerous topics that evening, with Ben telling Brad for the first time about the St. Adolphus assault and his later struggles. When he told Brad who the perpetrator was, Brad was unable to find words for several moments. Now he understood his father's concerns for his own safety and for that of his family. Clearly the Vatican would not let this information become public if they could at all help it and Brad became deeply concerned for his father's well-being. Before leaving, Ben lightened the mood by sharing with Brad a joke that had several twists and turns in it. They laughed and as they parted, agreed to talk soon.

At RAVOC's Chicago headquarters, excitement was mounting due to Ben's case. Brenda and Dan shared details of it – with Ben's permission of course -- with the remaining members of the organization's leadership team. They all agreed that his case had tremendous potential. While RAVOC's top priority was addressing and easing the suffering of victims, survivors, and their families, calling to account the Catholic Church was a close second and would help the organization's cause tremendously. Because of its purpose and mission coupled with modern communications capabilities, RAVOC was doing far more to focus attention on members of the clergy's egregious acts and to the Church's cover ups than any other movement in the Western World.

The public was becoming more and more aware of the lies of the Church as RAVOC and other organizations exposed the acts of pedophile priests abusing their power and those higher up skirting their responsibilities in order to cover up the disgraceful deeds. Unsuccessful in their efforts, of course, the Vatican and numerous dioceses around the globe took major hits in article after article in print and electronic news revealing the scandalous behavior of members of the Church's hierarchy. As the alliances between RAVOC and other advocacy groups strengthened, the Catholic Church's numbers continued to diminish and the Vatican's power weakened even further.

In Chicago, Brenda and Dan were receiving daily updates on Ben's case. They were pleased when they learned of the confirmations of assault by two more victims of Ben's old school – not that they were glad that others were assaulted, but that Ben's story now carried far more legitimacy with the church and – more importantly – the press. They suspected there would even be more victims identified as time went on. With Ben's permission, Attorney Sanders discussed the possibility of a settlement with Brenda, warning her of the possibility of a silence clause prohibiting public acknowledgement of Ben's abuse. They also were both aware that Ben opposed this, as he was determined to take on the Church, singlehandedly if need be. Sanders advised Brenda to sit tight and wait and see what might happen next before taking any action, but to be prepared to go to RAVOC's contacts at *The New York Times* and other media outlets, should the Church try to renege on its offer.

An ocean away, lights were burning at odd hours and the air was so thick with tension one could cut it with a knife. In the hallways of the Vatican, Pope Alexander IX pondered these recent events, acutely aware of the situation though desperately trying not to ascribe success to the plaintiff's efforts. As a defense, he feigned lack of interest and continued to downplay the accusations. He realized he was simply buying time and, as he had seen this play out so many times on his watch as head of the CDF, he knew his days were numbered. But still he maintained his innocence.

"I have seen this so many times, my son," he said to Cardinal Frenoso, the Secretary of State. "Those who wish us ill will stop at nothing to discredit us, finding someone that might have had a link in the past and buying their testimony, you see?"

Frenoso let it slide but after learning of the fourth such allegation, he was filled with rage. Loyal to the Vatican as an institution over all else, Frenoso broke protocol to growl angrily at the pontiff.

"You should have recused yourself at the Conclave and never even considered accepting the position as Pope!" Frenoso scowled. "The Church is already leaking from every pore! YOU! You never should have set foot in the Papal Chambers."

"So you believe these lies too?" Alexander said, shaking his head in seeming disappointment. Cardinal Frenoso was left to wonder, hoping against hope that the Pope was telling the truth after all. Were this regarding a traditionally Catholic country, Alexander's infallibility would never have come into question. But as the first American to become Pope, it was more convenient to discredit him than it was to swear eternal allegiance to the man. And the media outlets in the U.S. were all too happy to glom on to the newest scandal with a voracious appetite.

After Frenoso stormed out of his chamber, Alexander was morbid and worried, scrambling ferociously to gain any credible allies that he possibly could. Despite his cool outward demeanor he was unsuccessful, and discovered he was a pariah as news of the increasing number of allegations and fear of impending calamity spread around the compound. He considered hiring someone to assassinate the initial claimant who his sources identified as one Ben Clancy, but he knew that that would surely backfire in the world press if it ever got out that he, the Pope would orchestrate such an evil act. The name Ben Clancy did sound familiar, Mayron thought to himself. He had a vague memory of a beautiful, tall and lean young man in the prime of his youth ... He adjusted his robes and refocused his thoughts.

He was genuinely at a loss as to what to do and spent a large amount of time in solitude, away from the others. He was, in essence, totally ineffective as a leader from the very start. The pressure was growing and he didn't see any way out of this... Unless ...

Though on another continent, Ben kept tabs as best he could, setting up a Google alert for all news from Rome and reviewing it daily. He knew that the Vatican received official notification of his lawsuit, naming their elected leader as his perpetrator. But what he didn't know was that he, Ben, already exerted a tremendous amount of influence on that office from his humble rent-controlled apartment in Connecticut.

The call came through in mid-April on a Tuesday morning from Sanders' office with the time and confirmed location of the upcoming agreed upon meeting. Ben, the two attorneys and Jamie, along with representatives for the Vatican, the counsel for the Jesuits, Fr. Greg Camacho, and others that the church had selected would all meet the following Wednesday morning. The meeting would be held, not at Jesuit Headquarters as had been originally planned, but in a conference room in Attorney O'Donnell's office.

Ben was fully prepared and Attorney Sanders made sure of it. He also made Ben acutely aware of what was at stake. That was unnecessary, however, as Ben knew full well.

After a lengthy telephone conversation with Paul Adams, Ben spent the next several days engaging his neighbors in conversation but never letting on about his situation. To them, he appeared happy, productive, and entirely normal. He had dinner with Jamie on Saturday night at a local restaurant and updated her on the looming meeting.

"This is bigger than I thought," said Jamie, "and you certainly deserve a generous settlement," she told Ben. Ben didn't tell her that he was thinking of rejecting any settlement that called for further silence and secrecy from the church. To him it was tantamount to a bribe and he'd come too far to allow that. As he had learned many times during his lifetime, he would simply have to play this out and see where it would lead. He knew he had a strong shot at making the Pope and his old school pay for the enormous suffering he had endured, but he had also gained a lot of strength as a person and he was not about to play this hand foolishly.

On Sunday he drove into the city and met with Paul Adams. Since it was such a gorgeous day they met at the Cloisters at Fort Tryon Park, an irony that wasn't lost on either of them. Ben gave Paul a disk with the manuscript on it and gave him contact information for both Brad and Kelly.

"Just in case," Ben said.

Paul looked sharply at Ben.

"Ben, I'm really glad you've gamed this situation out to its possible conclusions," Paul said.

"Gamed?" Ben looked confused.

"You know, planned for any possibility. Not that I expect it would ever come to that, but it is better to be prepared for any eventuality," Paul said. "And it's clear to me you are."

Ben nodded and shrugged.

"Not that I think it would ever go that far. Clearly the Vatican realizes you are one of several victims …"

"Yes, thank God, if anything happened to me, there're others to expose him – and draw a link to whatever happened to me as well," Ben said and smiled wryly. "See, I guess I really have gamed this thing!"

They walked a while and Paul explained to Ben the plan he had formulated. It may not be warranted, but if things played out as they both expected, there might be need for a "Plan B," as Paul had mentioned some time back. "I just have to research a couple of final details to make sure it's fully legal," Paul explained.

On Wednesday morning, Jamie and Ben drove to Manhattan under gray skies. The air was cool and damp and there was a prediction for storms later in the day. Ben shivered slightly, both from the chilly air and in anticipation of the day's events. They chatted at a low volume until they reached the West Side Drive, when Ben's blood pressure began its inevitable rise. The rest of the drive was in silence as Ben focused on the road ahead. Pulling into the public garage next to Sander's office, they parked the car and walked silently into the office building, went up to the expansive cherry wood and hunter green upholstered office and waited to be acknowledged.

An assistant called them back with a friendly tone and showed Ben and Jamie to the conference room, offering coffee or tea which they accepted, giving their preferences. A moment later she returned with dark green coffee mugs emblazoned with the law firm's logo. Since they had arrived several minutes early, they sipped their coffee for a few minutes, relaxing somewhat as the warm liquid enveloped them, before Sanders and his partner, Attorney O'Donnell entered the room.

There was an air of camaraderie and teamwork in the air as Ben introduced Jamie and they all exchanged greetings. There was also the unexpressed notion that they were all here to win, and win soundly. Attorney Sanders instructed Ben to relax and simply tell the truth. Ben was determined not to let himself get intimidated in any way, shape or form.

Some 20 minutes later the entourage representing the Jesuits and the Vatican appeared led by Attorney Demarest, a hard-nosed former Prosecutor from the Bronx. Ben wasn't sure what his role was as Demarest introduced the two priests from New York's Jesuit headquarters, Father Greg Camacho and his assistant, Father Nate Winsted whose limp handshake made Ben stifle a shiver of disgust. Winsted would be working this case full time for the defense team, Demarest explained.

Attorney O'Donnell spoke and greeted everyone. Father Camacho, serving as head representative for the Jesuits, followed suit and expressed his sincere hope that this would be handled "pastorally" and with dignity. As Camacho spoke, Sanders sized up the roomful of people and watched Ben, his client, most carefully. He was glad to see that Jamie had a protective hand rested on Ben's arm and was glad Ben had brought her. Ben was about to get grilled by some very skilled interrogators.

"Ben, I'm truly sorry for what you have allegedly experienced. I say allegedly because I'm sure you understand, until we verify every claim you make here today, as members of the defense team, we must go on the assumption that the incident might have happened. Until proven to our satisfaction, however, it is only alleged", Camacho said, smiling in a patronizing fashion as he looked down at Ben.

"So, when did you first realize that it was Pope Alexander, or Cardinal Mayron who allegedly assaulted you?" Camacho asked, the half-smile still on his face.

"It was a year ago, when I attempted to commit suicide," Ben said matter-of-factly.

"Help me out here, please, Ben." Camacho shot back. "Was *that* the reason you tried to harm yourself or was it after attempting to do so that the realization came to you."

"It was mainly after," Ben said. "At that point all I wanted was to heal and get my life back... I had to go through intensive treatment, therapy, and soul-searching. It was then that the recollection of the incident came flooding back to me."

"I see…" The attorney pumped him with question after question about details of the encounter, coming at Ben from different angles to repeat the same question, hoping Ben would get confused or reveal an inconsistency. Camacho watched Ben's face carefully as he spoke and a videotape set up by the defense team was also aimed at him. After some 15 minutes of questions about the incident itself, Camacho launched into questions about Ben's overall experience at St. Adolphus, his childhood, and his family life during that time. He commented about Ben's lengthy commute and probed his experience in navigating New York City as an innocent youth, observing that a young child making his way through Port Authority on his own was impressive.

"I shared the ride with my dad to Port Authority and met up with a fellow classmate at the transfer stop. We employed the buddy system the rest of the trip in," Ben said dryly, figuring Camacho was trying to probe him for other occasions of vulnerability and opportunities for abuse.

After exploring this subject matter for some time, Camacho went on to question Ben's mental health.

"I have been diagnosed with Manic Depression, also known as Bi-Polar Disorder," Ben said matter-of-factly. "I take Lithium daily to regulate my brain chemistry."

At this point, Sanders interrupted, noting that Ben's diagnosis could very well be the direct result of a traumatic incident that damages the brain.

"If necessary, we can produce expert witnesses to testify to that fact."

"That won't be necessary," Camacho said, cutting Sanders off.

"But if I might add," Ben said, "I researched the diagnosis after I accepted it and got my head around the fact that I'd be on medications for the rest of my life. And what Attorney Sanders said is absolutely true."

After probing Ben's pre-teen mental health and behavior identified no weaknesses, Camacho questioned Ben about his years of substance abuse.

"I've been a recovering alcoholic and haven't touched alcohol or any drugs for more than two decades now," Ben said with some pride in his voice.

"In fact, here," he dug into his pocket and pulled out a metal disc. "This is my 20-year coin. I keep it with me, a reminder of the war I fought, and my accomplishment of which I'm very proud."

"But for years you were in and out of hospitals, drunk tanks, even jail, right?" Camacho shot back at him now. His tone was sharper and his words fired more rapidly.

"It is called self-medicating," Ben said. "When one's life becomes too loathsome to bear, and too painful, one tries to escape and shut it out as best as possible, with whatever medication they can find. For me it was booze. And without question it was a result of the assault by Mayron."

Sanders was stifling a smile and Jamie patted Ben's hand in support.

"Until I was diagnosed and put on the right medications, I tried whatever I could to relieve the demons that were troubling me," Ben said. "I believe if you did your research well, you will see that the hospitalizations and jail time ended at that time – 1990."

Camacho asked Ben about his grades and why he left St. Adolphus. Ben explained that when the assault occurred he was too ashamed to speak about it to anyone, including his parents and siblings. "I went into a form of shock that began when I was raped," he said. Glad that Camacho went into this line of questioning, Ben went on.

"As a matter-of-fact, I recently received a copy of my transcripts from St. Adolphus and checked the school's disciplinary and education policy," he said and paused for effect. "Based on the information I received, my expulsion was falsified – a crime within a crime, you might say."

A smug smile spread across Ben's face as Camacho sat down.

"I'm done," he mumbled and turned to Demarest. "You want to ask him anything else?"

Camacho's co-counsel Demarest, the former prosecutor then grilled Ben, a snarl just below the surface of his pock-marked complexion. Adrenalin flowing now, Ben answered sharply, intelligently and factually, showing the defense that his story was based on facts and no amount of effort on their parts would shake his conviction.

After another hour of grilling by the cocky Demarest, Ben stopped answering, looked around and pounded his fist on the table several times to gain everyone's attention.

They all stared at him in stunned silence.

"I am the one here who was assaulted and I'll be damned if I will be put on trial for someone else's crime!" he said with fury.

Taken aback, Demarest acquiesced and turned his gaze to Camacho who nodded with a smile toward Sanders and asked if his team could have some time in private to deliberate. Ben and company stood and left the defense team in the conference room. Sanders guided Ben and his advocates into the employee lounge, motioning to the secretary to offer more beverages.

Each accepted bottled water and sipped as Sanders spoke.

"Ben, great job. I think they've come to the conclusion your allegations are truthful. They already have the documentation on the other incidents and I'm sure will probe those other victims for accuracy too. Your case is the strongest, though, and I'm confident they'll want to settle instead of dallying around to give us a chance to go class on them."

"Excuse me," Ben said, looking around, confused. "Class?"

"Class action," Sanders explained.

"Oh, right, I didn't think of that," Ben said, frowning as he realized this was another alternative.

Meanwhile, in the conference room, the mood was bleak.

"He's telling the truth and worse, makes for an engaging witness," Camacho summed up for the group who sat forward in their chairs. "It's not out in the public yet, but that threat is real and would do irreparable harm to St. Adolphus, our order, and the Pope as well."

Demarest knew it. Winsted knew it, and Father Camacho knew it. A few moments of pure speculative dialogue ensued with little result, but recognizing they were over a barrel, they agreed on their next moves. Putting his game face back on, Camacho peeked his head into the reception area and nodded to the secretary who entered the break room and indicated to Ben's group that the defense team was ready for Ben and his legal representatives to join them again in the conference room. Ben's stomach churned but he tried hard not to show it.

Seated once again, Jamie squeezed Ben's arm as Camacho and company acknowledged that Ben appeared to have been abused grievously and they were determined to make amends. Camacho then asked Ben to maintain silence on the matter and produced a document for him to sign. Ben glanced over at Sanders momentarily and then, matter-of-factly refused, pushing the document away from him. As he did, he sent up a silent prayer of thanks to Paul for recommending that maneuver. Ben told them that it was unnecessary and, sitting back and folding his arms in dismissal, confidently wished them all a good day. The defense team, dumbfounded, looked at one another, stood silently, and left the room without salutations. O'Donnell and Sanders stood to show them out. Ben and Jamie seated, stayed behind. "You handled that beautifully, Ben!" O'Donnell said as he returned to the room. "They have a lot to think about."

"So do we, and yes you did, Ben," Sanders said, eyeing Ben with a newfound respect. "Let's give it a break, but stay alert and on top of this every step of the way. Go home and get some rest and I am sure we'll have a response soon."

Jamie and Ben returned to the car and drove to Connecticut, lost in their separate thoughts. Jamie spoke very little, but Ben still needed her very much as an ally. She had begun to see things from Ben's point of view and realized it was no longer just about the money and the settlement. It was becoming something more for her, too. It was about truth, about justice and, ultimately, about her former husband's self-worth. She didn't see the big picture as clearly as Ben did, but Ben's flat out denial of a settlement alerted her that there was much more going on here than a simple law suit.

The ride back was long and tiring, but they ended up going out for a bite together to cap off the day. Jamie was beginning to trust Ben more and saw that he really was a good man, despite his shortcomings. And following his testimony today, she realized even most of his flaws had a rational explanation and it wasn't truly Ben's fault. As for Jamie, Ben knew full well that she was far from perfect, too, but that she was still the love of his life. Ideally, he saw them back together again when this was all over, but for now, he could not afford the distraction a physical relationship would bring.

He dropped Jamie off after dinner, kissed her lightly on the cheek and said goodnight. Then he went home to his nightly paperwork. Once that was done, he made several calls to update family and trusted RAVOC advocates, saving a thank you call to Paul Adams for last.

"It never would have occurred to me that I didn't have to sign that!" he said. "And as much as I appreciate what Sanders does, he's a lawyer and didn't advise me that I didn't have to sign it either. I owe you, Paul!"

"Just remind Carl what help I am being, OK?" he said, smiling at the other end of the phone line.

The next day Ben got a brief follow up call from Sanders who reiterated how well he had handled himself under pressure. "Let's just wait and see what they come up with next before we make a move. In the meantime, I will be researching international case law in the event we want to file anything in Rome." He followed this with encouragement to Ben to be brave and remain clear-minded.

Ben knew at this point that most everything had been set into motion and that there really wasn't much for him to do from here on in – except continue to speak his truth and eventually publish his book. He felt freer than he ever had in his adult life because he had stood up, told his story, and was holding his perpetrators accountable for their misdeeds. He had always insisted on being as honest as he could, so it never occurred to him to ask himself why he should have been the one to stand up against the Church. He knew that there was no going back, but he also knew there were others, countless others who would one day stand up as well. They needed him strong right here and now to pave the way.

He wasn't sure if this was a good sign or not. Paul suggested in one of their newly established weekly telephone calls that it meant both the Vatican and Jesuits here in the states were buying time and perhaps looking for weaknesses in Ben's and the other victim's claims. At Paul's suggestion, Ben called Attorney Sanders' office several times, but there was no news. The attorney did not return his calls, but did send a nice Birthday card over the Easter Holidays. Ben tried to keep a positive attitude and received calls of support from Jamie, Kelly, Carl, and of course, his team of allies within RAVOC.

At the same time, Kelly was putting out feelers in the publishing world to see if any agents might be interested in Ben's fictionalized story. She sent the manuscript to a couple of publishers' development editors as well. They both knew it was a waiting game and realized it was better for them to hold tight until Ben resolved his claim with the Vatican and Jesuits before signing any deals. They reasoned, however, and Paul agreed, that it wouldn't be bad to start creating a buzz and perhaps even generate a rumor or two about such an upcoming product.

Outwardly, the Roman Catholic Church was operating as usual, and Pope Alexander IX said the annual Easter Mass, and performed other public appearances. But within the walls of the Vatican, however, especially after Easter week, there was nothing but consternation, hand wringing and a whole ton of confusion.

Artur Manois, a reporter with Agency France Press, had been following the crisis in the Roman Catholic Church for nearly a decade. He had stumbled across rumors of a major suit involving the head of the Vatican, the Pope himself, through some of his sources across the Atlantic. He sped by TGV through the hills of France to Rome and questioned several Cardinals that he had interviewed in preceding years on background. The reaction was a cold silence, but that did not stop Manois. He dug deeper and guessed that the truth would be revealed in the near future across the ocean, in the heart of New York City.

Members of the College of Cardinals were in heated talks over who the next Pope should be, and what to do with the current Vicar. Although Pope Alexander IX had not initiated it and refused to discuss it, there was much talk within Vatican City of his resignation. He made few appearances and though the allegations about his past had not yet been made public, it was only a matter of time before they would be. That is, unless by some incredible stroke of luck the parties settled and the plaintiffs agreed to keep the allegations off the record.

Alexander had little time to enjoy the palatial surroundings he previously enjoyed, nor the immense wealth he was now in charge of. As Cardinal James Mayron of New York City, he had dined with the rich and the famous, including many notable politicians as well as the President of the United States. He had a small fortune at his disposal as head of the New York Archdiocese, and almost unlimited power over the millions of Catholics in his charge back then. What would they think of him now if they knew the truth? This very real scenario gnawed at him throughout every waking minute, until now, when just a few weeks into his Papacy, he was turning into a shell of a man.

He toyed with the idea of setting up a dummy account and filtering ample funds into it for his eventual demise and departure as Pope, but he knew by now that it would not go undetected. Truth is, he was deeply afraid of what awaited him. Sure, he still had supporters back in the states, some of whom were very powerful, but if the abuse and pending lawsuits became common knowledge, even they would turn their backs on him. Thoughts of suicide flashed into his mind at random times during the day and especially at night as he found it increasingly difficult to sleep. Over and over again he asked himself if he could indeed remain the Pope and still save face for the Church, which, though he no longer loved it, he still owed his livelihood to it. One of the most important precepts of being Pope was the doctrine of infallibility bestowed upon the individual in that position. He clung to that now but realized it was ultimately a hoax, at least as far as he was concerned, and that he was indeed perceived as quite fallible. His great hope was that focus on this entire sordid affair would soon be ended forever, however, he knew the chances of that occurring were slim indeed.

He neither ate nor slept and lost the many friends and allies he had cultivated over the years in Rome. How did he get here he wondered, reflecting back on his childhood and teen years and then to his years as Headmaster. Physically weak but academically gifted as a child, he was encouraged to join the priesthood from a very early age. It was during a weekend retreat that the sexual proclivities that led him to molest powerless young men and boys came to him. Like many sexual predators, he was a victim himself early on. But he enjoyed it! And sought it out, and for this reason, the priesthood was a natural fit for him, although not all priests enjoyed the sexual companionship of young boys or other men. He thought fondly back to his days in St. Mary's seminary, and smiled, gently recalling his several romances of that time.

The noonday chimes brought him back to the present and the Pope drew encouragement from the fact that although he never had to work in the corporate world, he did understand wealth and power. And, like the infamous Machiavelli, he was determined to hold onto his own if at all possible. The thought made him stand a bit taller and, scanning his memory for allies, he knew the one person left that he could count on was Cardinal Joseph Ramsey. The Archbishop of Washington, D.C., Ramsey enjoyed a great deal of popularity among the European members of the College and had been a dear (dear!) friend to Alexander since the days the two were roommates in St. Mary's seminary way back when. Yes, the Pope thought, he could definitely count on Ramsey.

With a plan starting to form in his mind, Pope Alexander called for a meeting with Cardinal Ramsey on the following day and looked to play the only trump card he had left. At the last minute, he also asked that Cardinal Bernardo Bertolucci of Milan join them. Alexander had befriended Bertolucci when he was first introduced to life in the Vatican several years before and there was some amount of trust between them. Just how much Alexander would soon find out.

Still head of the New York Archdiocese about the time news of the first sex scandals broke, Mayron worked very closely under then Cardinal Reichsinger, the head of the Sacred CDF. As a team, the two wielded enormous power over the whole of the Catholic hierarchy with regard to media relations dealing with the exploding sexual allegations. When Reichsinger became Pope, Cardinal Mayron took over the reins of the CDF, and Cardinal Bertolucci, a fellow conservative, served as his deputy.

Mayron and Bertolucci maintained close ties throughout the last few years, recognizing the imperative of keeping the Church afloat at any cost. With so many abuse claims piling up, and with all the bad press, it meant a huge investment of time and effort on both their parts. Now, Alexander/ Mayron knew Bertolucci would be eager to serve in any way that he could to protect the Church. When the summons arrived, Bertolucci acknowledged the secretary who came to him with instructions that he was to meet in the Pope's Chambers the next morning at 7 a.m. He sent the secretary away with his affirmation.

The hefty Uduno-born Bertolucci knew well of the latest scandal involving the Pope, and knew this would be his most difficult test ever. To succeed, Bertolucci had to put aside the irony and feelings of betrayal he felt after having worked with Mayron for so many years. They had both worked to investigate the disgraceful behavior of other members of the church who had done the very thing Mayron was accused of doing. Whatever ties the two still maintained would soon be put to the test in mortal fashion.

The Pope awoke at 5 the next morning, went through his usual pre-dawn routine but eliminated his ornamental attire for the meeting with the designated cardinals in his Chambers. For this meeting, he dressed humbly as a common priest, largely to garner sympathy and to create the illusion of equality. The two prelates were waiting when the Pope entered and greeted them. At this point, he had two thoughts. First, he regretted not holding individual meetings with each where he might arm-twist and persuade them personally, using blackmail over Ramsey if necessary, and reason over Bertolucci. Alexander was thinking only of his own power now, and any other player in his arena was merely a pawn to be moved to and fro.

Totally numb inside, the Pope suspected he had little time left in office if events proceeded as they had been unfolding. The meeting of the three men went on for over two hours, as the so-called men of faith tried to look at the problem from every possible angle. As professionals of the highest order, both Ramsey and Bertolucci kept their disgust and mounting hatred of Alexander to themselves. They realized they had to do something or the Vatican, and their very ways of life would be permanently changed – and not for the better.

At one point, out of desperation for his beloved church, Cardinal Bertolucci offered to "take care of the problem" by eliminating Ben Clancy via some of the church's contacts in the underworld. Cardinal Ramsey and the Pope quickly rejected the offer noting that the attorneys would carry on in Ben's absence. They carefully scrutinized Clancy's dossier -- including his divorce decree and notes from the private investigator the Jesuits had immediately contracted to keep tabs on him after Sanders' first call. In the end, they determined that they'd use Vatican funds to make Clancy a settlement offer far greater than any ever reached with a plaintiff before. It would be one he could not refuse, they were confident, and in exchange it would mean his silence.

After they left his chambers, Alexander took his rosary, sank into the burgundy leather club chair near the fireplace and prayed for some time, hoping this would work. He feared it wouldn't though, as there were other victims identified and these might not be silenced as easily. Ashamed and filled with regret over his past indiscretions now, Alexander realized there was no way to salvage his credibility and sanctity, even if he, as the Pope, was technically infallible.

Losing count on the rosary beads, he dropped them to his lap and began to reflect. He felt like the loneliest man on the face of the earth, if he could be called a man at all. He accepted that his entire life was built on a sham and he had flaunted unearned power for decades over blind and unsuspecting gentle people who longed only for solace from the cruel mishaps of the world. And worse, he now realized, the sexual assaults he had committed over the young boys he had molested had aroused him because of the power he wielded over them. Now, the tables had turned and the entire weight of his actions lay on his shoulders. He begged for this to be over, but knew he brought it on himself, and no confessional in the world could ever absolve him now.

Cardinal Ramsey contacted Father Camacho in New York relating to him the huge sum offered. Camacho then passed on this information to his associate, the attorney for the Church, Brock Demarest and they agreed Camacho would convey the offer to Sanders insisting on a quick resolution and full silence. As always, the Church could not bear any more scandals, though it might already be too late.

In the meantime, Sanders' team identified a fourth victim of the former headmaster, and there was no telling how many more there were, though it was presumed that some would be dead by now. When word of his investigative team's findings reached Ben's attorney, he knew he could pursue this entire affair full out and win decisively. It also meant the threat of a class action case!

As Sanders' team researched the matter further, they learned that only two of the four other survivors had signed on with Sanders and O'Donnell. The other two victims secured the legal representation of Ed Stillwater, a well-known attorney who had less experience litigating clergy abuse cases but had garnered big sums for plaintiffs in several product liability matters. As soon as they'd signed on, Stillwater approached Jesuit headquarters with his two plaintiff's cases. Father Camacho was preparing to approach Sanders with the offer relayed to him by Ramsey when Stillwater's call came in. As he picked up the phone, Camacho feared the worst. He knew this entire situation would rock the Vatican if it were to come to light, but there was little he could do about it. Handing out quick settlements with ironclad secrecy clauses was the only way to deal with this mess, or so they all hoped.

The first settlement of $1,000,000 was reached within seven days of being filed by Stillwater. Demarest, the seasoned prosecutor, realized the precariousness of their situation and had Camacho prepare the documents and extend a ludicrously generous offer, ready to "roll over" for Stillwater's victims, hoping this competing attorney didn't learn of Sanders' multiple cases.

"Get a representative of the Vatican over here immediately and as discreetly as possible to serve as liaison for the claims!" Demarest commanded.

He fired off other rapid recommendations to Father Camacho who realized the enormity of the situation and spent countless hours handholding Stillwater until the Vatican liaison arrived and the cases were summarily dispensed with.

Realizing the Vatican was taking advantage of secrecy requirements, Sanders stewed as he learned the case of the first victim had been disposed of so rapidly. Still, he knew there were at least three more complainants to deal with, not counting Ben. Sanders did his best to persuade his other two clients – independently of course – to hold out before signing in case something else became public. They were both desperate for the money and uninterested in the attention such a claim would likely garner, however, and he was obligated to convey to them the overwhelmingly generous cash settlement the co-defendants were offering. Like Stillwater's remaining complainant, they accepted quickly and agreed to the legal stipulation that silence be maintained in the entire affair.

When reviewing Ben's case over a celebratory highball after the last of those plaintiffs settled, both Father Camacho and Attorney Demarest agreed that they were dealing with an entirely different breed in Clancy. Recalling his preliminary deposition, they realized he made a very strong case for himself, drawing a link – however subjective – between his abuse and later mental health issues, and worse, hinting at collusion between the then-headmaster and others within St. Adolphus. And they were sure Sanders – a brilliant litigator – would find countless professionals to make any jury on earth believe those linkages were indisputable. But going that route was the last thing they or the Pope, for that matter, wanted to see.

Worse, though, this Clancy fellow was the type that would shout from the rooftops about the assault and more than likely shake loose the memories and tongues of other complainants as well. That was something neither St. Adolphus nor the Vatican could afford.

"Remember how he refused to sign the docs at the deposition?" Demarest said. "He's got serious balls."

"Controlled rage might be a better term for what his true feelings are," Camacho countered. "Remember, of the other four victims who settled, three were still mired in booze and drug abuse hazes and were not savvy enough to cause problems. The other victim, in treatment for pancreatic cancer with only a few weeks to live, was simply happy to settle for the $1,500,000 that he could leave to his family when he died."

Demarest nodded and downed his scotch, shaking his glass to signal he needed a refill. Camacho obliged, clinking two ice cubes into the glass first.

The next day Camacho contacted Sanders.

"Look, I'll grant you that your client Clancy is an extraordinary plaintiff and would have done extremely well in court," Camacho said. "But you must realize the prospect of a class action suit is off the table and it's in yours and his best interest to settle now."

"I'll get back to you," Sanders said. The investigative team had been unsuccessful in identifying any other potential victims and he was inclined to agree. But it was ultimately up to his client. In a closed door meeting with O'Donnell later that afternoon, the two lawyers agreed it would be far better for the firm's balance sheet to close Ben's case, collect their fees, and go about their business.

"I'll present the offer and explain the situation to him," Sanders said, "but I have a feeling he's in this for blood."

In Vatican City, Cardinals Ramsey and Bertolucci telephoned each other from their private offices, recognizing it would be most unwise to be seen together. Neither felt overly optimistic about the emerging crisis in New York City, and both were convinced they were seeing the waning days of the reign of Pope Alexander IX. The two prelates still had futures to consider and aligning themselves with Alexander, no matter how pure the motive, would taint each of their long term statuses. Ramsey was at the point of cutting all ties with the Pope, former lovers or not, and Bertolucci was on the fence, still hoping the victims' silence could be bought and that somehow they might salvage Alexander's papacy – for the good of the Vatican.

Spring was here in its fullness, along with the crocuses and forsythia in the Northeast. Ben absolutely loved this time of year and took advantage of it, going for lengthy walks alone or with Jamie or Brad. He had settled into a comfortable routine as a highly creative individual, writing, composing, and playing and his website was generating modest ad revenues. Right now, life offered him all the freedom he could ask for and despite the cloud of what had happened to him, he was in an optimistic frame of mind. Not only that, he was very well prepared for what was to come.

Jerry Sanders called him the week after Easter with the $14,000,000 settlement offer. "That would mean $8.5 million for you, after the firm's fees are deducted," he said.

Ben asked Sanders' opinion and the lawyer matter-of-factly pointed out the pros and cons, making it very clear to Ben that he would never be able to talk about the situation again to anyone under the terms of the contract.

"No, I am sorry, that is unacceptable," Ben said, determination lowering the timber of his voice to a growl. "I will not agree to a settlement that silences me. I will not let those bastards go scot free."

Sanders hesitated for a moment and drew in a patient breath.

"Ben, that's what this legal case is all about and it would be unrealistic of you to refuse a secrecy clause. That's unfortunately how this is done," Sanders said, choosing his words carefully.

"I realize that's the usual way," Ben said, "but I'll be damned if I sell my silence like this. Look, I'm sorry if I've mislead you into thinking ..."

Sanders realized where he was going with his comment and cut him off. A skilled negotiator, he knew Ben's position was very solid, but he was sure he could find some common ground on which to reach an agreement.

"We do need to counter, Ben," he then said hopefully.

"Well then, tell them $100,000,000 and no chance for silence!" Ben was abrupt, almost curt, but determined to take charge.

The lawyer cleared his throat and told Ben that he would present the offer, but that he didn't think they would comply. They finished their conversation and Ben found himself alone in his study. He sank into his armchair and pondered.

In a way, he didn't care at all about the money. For the last twenty years he had lived honest and free, as unencumbered as he could from material desires and needs. With all his heart, he believed in his own divine purpose, his karma. He was not about to sell out to a corrupt organization he saw begging for mercy.

When Ben first came forward, and during the interviews with Camacho and Demarest, he described what had happened to him as a spear being thrust right through the center of his soul. Only he knew the darkness he had lived through, the incredible nightmare he had endured day after agonizing day. The difference between himself and the four others who had settled, he thought, was that he genuinely cared about the plight and suffering of other abuse victims throughout the world. He saw the bigger picture. He knew what powerlessness was and that when he was raped he was an extremely helpless victim. Now, he was taking his power back. He would not be swayed in the slightest by anything less than a full and enduring justice. He was prepared.

Chapter 15
The Wait

Ben fully supported the work of his friends in RAVOC whether it was in lobbying for stricter laws against predators in order to gain justice for victims and survivors, or in its actions with the media bringing higher-ups from the Church heirarchy to justice. He often included links to new information on his website and tweeted to his several hundred followers about these cases. He knew RAVOC was an organization he could rely on to speak the truth and also to shed light on the dark dealings of the Catholic Church and other institutions.

One trail he thought worth investigating but not directly in RAVOC's purview was the Vatican Bank's massive financial holdings. He tried to point out to RAVOC's leaders the necessity of getting a handle on the financial arm because, as he knew well, and as RAVOCs' leaders came to realize, the Cardinals and Bishops as well as the Pope were constructing a metaphoric moat around their assets in light of the huge settlements and judgments mounting against them.

PART FOUR

Power Play

Chapter 16
Into Action

Sanders contacted Camacho the next day with the counter offer. He did not defend his client's position to the opposing attorney. In fact, after giving it more thought the night before, he accepted Ben's decision and began to understand and appreciate his motive and his approach, deeply impressed by the man's grit and determination. Heavily involved in the fight for victim's rights for over 20 years, money was not Sanders' only motivating factor either. Still, there were business realities to contend with and he would have to reconcile all this with his partner, O'Donnell.

The air around the Vatican was thick with gloom and irony. The fact was this once great institution, the most powerful landholder on the face of the earth who answered to no one, was now hiding behind its stone and marble exteriors and gasping for breath. This was all because the current Pope – who was the institution's previous chief fixer when it came to clergy abuse scandals – was about to be brought down by such a scandal himself. This was not lost on the majority of those wearing the scarlet cap.

They were aware an international revolution of sorts had taken place in the past 10 years, and the Vatican was at the crosshairs of this war... Law enforcement officials worldwide were no longer giving leeway to the Church as they began to hold religious pedophiles accountable as criminals. Other suspicious acts were being investigated by Interpol and other authorities as well – money laundering, corruption, even murder – and these 'other' crimes were, of course, being covered in the news. Most troubling of all were those in the international community who were calling for revocation of the Church's standing as an independent sovereign entity. No one in the Vatican needed to be told what the implications of that would be...

Alexander could barely eat or sleep and was visited only by his doctor, a few nuns who were also nurses, a couple of priests on his immediate staff, and an occasional Cardinal vying for a signature regarding his own particular province. He was on a heavy dose of antidepressants and sleeping pills because of all he faced. Most power at this point lay with the Secretary of State who gave orders to the Vatican Bank's chief administrator, Bishop Nardonne, that any transaction involving the Pope must first be reviewed by the Secretary before being carried out.

In one of his more lucid moments, Alexander realized he was about to be scrutinized as never before and no longer had the luxury of feeling and behaving "above the Law." He was somewhat mollified when he recalled from his earlier days as head of CDF that the U.S. statute of limitations would prevent his being charged and tried. But that didn't help him here in Italy. As the revelations came to light, confirmed by those other victims' allegations, he lost all dignity and standing, not to mention respect here in the confines of Vatican City. As for being an admirable Great Father and Governor of Men, Pope Alexander was absolutely impotent and hardly even a figurehead. The only legacy he would leave, he feared, was one of shame and ignominy.

He received his information by courier as he could trust neither telephone nor email in matters of privacy. In the waning days of his papacy, he summoned one last burst of braggadocio and asked to meet with the College of Cardinals the following Tuesday, ostensibly to discuss the Church's policies regarding two matters: women entering the priesthood and contraception. He would move from discussion of those two policy issues to his own situation, and, citing his health, would propose to the College of Cardinals that he step down and return to his former post as head of the CDF.

The meeting was scheduled for the following Tuesday at 12 Noon in the Vatican dining hall. There was much talk among the members of the College of Cardinals noting the inadequacy and impotence of the current Pontiff with a great deal of dismay. A few thought that they should not take him for granted, that he could still rebound from the shroud of dark secrets that hovered over him. Most others scoffed and felt that there was no way out of this except to get rid of the Pope.

The whispers continued for several days before the meeting as the Cardinals wondered what he might say. Jesuit Headquarters in New York relieved Alexander somewhat with the good news that four settlements had been reached with his victims and that secrecy had so far been maintained. However, they noted that one holdout, Ben Clancy, remained and was not eager to settle in silence as the others were.

Alexander's future, and for that matter, the Vatican's lay in the hands of this one American survivor of the Pope's sexual assault years ago.

Ben was mindful of the unsought power that he now wielded. He got a call from RAVOC's leader, Brenda Lawson who would be in Manhattan over the next few days, and wanted to meet with Ben. They agreed to get together on Friday around midday at a café she knew on West 57th. Ben maintained his weekly telephone conversations with Paul and arranged for a meeting with him after lunch with Brenda.

Ben reflected on this Godsend of a guy and observed that Paul was investing a great deal of time in his case. Curious, Ben wondered what he was hoping to get out of it. He tried to probe Carl for more information about Paul, but Carl was as elusive as ever. It came from his many years serving with the State Department overseas, Ben thought to himself. Though Carl's official title was "Diplomat," Ben always suspected there was more that Carl never shared. A common joke among the rest of the family members was that Carl was a spook. Hard to believe, since Carl was so nerdy and wonkish. But then, maybe that's what made him such a great spy if he was one – no one would suspect him!

Attorney Sanders was not exactly certain which direction he should take in Ben's case at this point. He was usually adept at guiding people towards a predetermined objective, but here he was not exactly sure what that objective was or should be. On the one hand, he could maneuver for a sizable settlement, close the deal and walk away. But Clancy was stubborn and it looked like he wasn't in it just for the money. What's more, Sanders was becoming drawn in on Ben's quest for full accountability by the Church.

Sanders knew he could handle O'Donnell whichever direction they decided to take. The Vatican would of course attempt to bury them in paperwork and filings, delaying the case from here to the next decade and then some. It would undoubtedly mean a massive amount of resources tied up in this one victim's suit. But he'd remind O'Donnell that if need be, they could get investors to handle trial expenses, like Lawcash, if it went that far. More and more it looked like his client was determined to take it to the mat, and deep down part of the seasoned attorney looked forward to the fight!

His ethical obligation to his client aside, Sanders was impressed by Ben and deeply admired his honesty, courage and integrity. When calculating a settlement figure, he factored into his case the enormous damage done to Ben, what Ben might have accomplished had this drastic occurrence never happened, and the fact that his abuser was the Pope. Probing Ben's background, the attorney realized Clancy's whole family was extraordinary. One, a retired diplomat, one, a national champion athlete, one, manager of a five-star hotel, and more. No weak links in the Clancy family – until you got to Ben. And that's why this case was becoming so important, Sanders realized. The victim was an extraordinary individual in his own right, deserved his day in court, and could have – who knows, could have become president one day had his time at St. Adolphus not been abruptly cut short in the manner which it was! Years of training prepared Sanders for the long haul and the bigger picture, something he could clearly begin to imagine and – more importantly, believe in. Sanders accepted that he'd be content either way. Though he knew that if they kept going and declined the offer, in Rome there would be a great deal of upheaval behind the heavy drapes and stone walls.

Like any great classic tragedy, the drama heightened daily in the Vatican. At the Pope's meeting the following Tuesday, he addressed the Cardinals present, discussing the doctrinal topics on the agenda, and called for a renewal of faith and a real commitment to fundamental dogma. He then segued into the much anticipated discussion about his situation and its implications for his future Papacy.

"You are all aware by now of the allegations made against my good name and against our church," He started and paused, soberly looking around the room at his colleagues. "There are those who wish us harm, who want to destroy this great institution, the Roman Catholic Church. To them I say, 'God is with us, and as Satan urges you on in your unholy quest for money, I still pray for your soul."

There was a murmur through the crowd as the Pope continued.

"I will not dignify the allegations with a response but want to warn you all here with me today that this is a very ugly, dark time for our Church and I will do whatever is necessary to protect it. That is all I care to say on this matter at this time. Thank you and God be with you all"

He turned to leave the massive room when a voice cried out.

"That's all?"

Eyes turned to Cardinal Luiz Montevain from Brazil.

"I am sorry, Your Holiness, I did not mean to speak out of turn," the stunned Cardinal said somewhat sheepishly. "But I believe we need to address these allegations further right here and now as the repercussions affect us all."

Many in the room expressed agreement in an atypical display of lack of discipline in the usually highly structured meetings. The mini-revolt was quickly quelled when Secretary of State Cardinal Frenoso, moved to stand next to the Pope.

"That will be all, gentlemen," he said with an air of finality that no one questioned. All got up to exit but as they filed out of the room, several of the Cardinals hung back to discuss what had just happened. The majority of Cardinals had already written Alexander off, while the other half were loyal to the Papacy at all costs. It was clear that several were positioning themselves, building alliances, and vying for power should the call come, including the ever-ambitious Montevain who had been on the media's short-list of likely successors to Boniface before Mayron was named. It was clear, though, that all who wore the red cassock were in the dark as to what outcome would prevail. Prayers were offered up, special novenas said, and some faithful to the institution even fasted, hoping the Almighty would intercede and this crisis would go away.

Pope Alexander and his staff made preparations for an international news conference the following Friday, via Vatican Radio. He would take no questions from the press and the words would be very carefully scripted. Alexander had carried on through some very troubling times as Cardinal of New York and, whether it was the antidepressants or simply his adrenaline flowing, he somehow found renewed energy to go on with pretenses for as long as possible, thinking that perhaps this would all miraculously blow over!

On Friday, via Vatican Radio, Pope Alexander gave his address, reaffirming the stance Boniface had taken before him on women entering the priesthood. In no uncertain terms, he stated that anyone involved in the ordination of women as priests would be excommunicated. He also repeated the Church's stance on contraception, that using any form of contraception was indeed a grave sin. Since there were to be no questions, the address was simply window-dressing and a photo opportunity cleverly showing the Pope healthy and in control – despite rumors circulating to the contrary.

AFP reporter Manois was there, of course and covered the official statement before meeting separately with aides to two Cardinals he understood were disgruntled over the recent occurrences. From the first aide he garnered the fact that the College of Cardinals was still being kept in line as it were. However, from the second aide, he learned that several of the Cardinals had agreed to a secret meeting to consider their options. He knew he would be unable to get into the meeting, but there might be a way to at least get some more information about what the breakaway Cardinals were considering... He got the names of four other disgruntled Cardinals and hurriedly began contacting their aides.

Ben heard of the Pope's declaration and almost puked. He felt very strongly about the dangers of overpopulation and the essential need for contraception and had for decades, since reading Rachel Carson's <u>Silent Spring</u> when it was first published in the early 1970's. As for women remaining ineligible to become priests, the Catholic Church remains in the dark ages, he thought, and, like the Taliban and other extremist faiths, clearly maintains its unhealthy fear of women.

After his address, Alexander retreated to Castle Gandolfo again, to get away for a few days and ponder his next moves. He invited Cardinals Ramsey and Bertolucci to join him along with several members of his staff. Bodyguards from the Swiss Guard drove him and watched over him, professionally oblivious of the impending scandal. The ride up was quiet, with the Pope and his two Cardinals lost in their own thoughts.

Upon arrival, they all went to their separate quarters to freshen up and pray. They dined together on fish, pasta and bread, accompanied by a local wine. The estate's chef was lured from a Michelin-rated restaurant two years earlier and all who ate his fare were grateful. As the diners stood to depart for their rooms, the Pope asked Ramsey and Bertolucci to meet him the next morning at 7 a.m. They didn't have to guess at the reason.

As the estate in the mountains of Italy grew dark, across the ocean Brenda Lawson and Attorney Sanders met with Ben Clancy in the law firm's New York conference room. The location had been changed from Brenda's intended café to Sanders' office after he called her to suggest the three meet. Each agreed it was a good idea.

During the drive down from Connecticut, Ben did some serious thinking. He felt confident that he was on the right track and had a good support team surrounding him. He also thought of the danger to himself in exposing the Pope as his predator, but trusted in his heart and in his gut that he would be safe. He wrote the fears off, as he had been doing lately, as being melodramatic and perhaps a bit paranoid.

As usual, Ben was the first to arrive at the office. The law firm's secretary showed him to the conference room and offered him coffee which he gratefully accepted. Brenda came in a few minutes later and, never having met her in person before, Ben was taken by her petite, but striking beauty and gentle demeanor. He wasn't fooled, though, as he knew her to be a relentless advocate when it came to her battles on behalf of victims and survivors. She, like Ben, had swallowed the entire lie growing up and spent the last 20 years formulating her own rational set of principles that genuinely worked for her.

Attorney Sanders showed up a few minutes later, hair askew and somewhat out of breath. "Sorry I'm late." He apologized quickly and left it at that. They all knew why they were there and knew as well that they were definitely on the same team, and most certainly on the same page.

The three of them discussed in detail every facet of Ben's case that they could think of. Brenda shed light on activities RAVOC was leading across the states and from its European offices as well. She also mentioned engaging in some serious talks with high ranking officials from the United Nations regarding the Vatican. There was now a move in place to prosecute the Vatican for Crimes against Humanity, in light of the sex abuse cases around the globe. Others in the international community were hoping to see the Sovereignty of the Vatican abolished altogether one day in the near future. Her information was welcome but wasn't news since both Sanders and Ben kept abreast of the events in the Vatican with intense interest.

Brenda then told Ben she was considering him to serve as RAVOC's liaison to the U.N. This would be in conjunction with Attorneys Sanders and O'Donnell, and also with the help of the international community. Before offering him the post formally, she would have to vet him, she explained, to see if he was up to it. They all knew how different stresses can trigger PTSD. Brenda did not want to lose Ben or see him scarred any further, but she knew he'd be a valuable addition to their organization, from all she'd heard and learned about him. Ben assured them both he was honored to be considered and certain he could handle the job, but made it clear that this pending case with the Jesuits was his most important priority.

Sanders then spoke, updating Ben and, with his permission, Brenda, on Ben's case. They had been unable to find any other victims to testify against the Pope, and since those other four cases had settled, there was no chance to turn this into a Class Action case. Both Sanders and Brenda knew Ben was adamant about not signing away his right to speak out about what had happened, so that part of the meeting was brief. Simply put, the Vatican and St. Adolphus had yet to respond to Ben's counter offer.

Ben left the law firm's office on his own since Brenda had other RAVOC-related issues to discuss with Sanders. Rather than driving, he took a cab uptown to meet Paul. They were to meet at a great little Russian eatery on West 54th. Ben was looking forward to some good hearty fare. But he was even more eager to finally ask Paul why he was putting so much time into Ben's case.

Chapter 17
Critical Mass

Ben met Paul at the entrance to Uncle Vanya's and the two entered together. They were able to grab a corner table by a window and promptly ordered. After the waitress left, Ben began.

"Paul, you've got to know, I really appreciate all you've done for me, man. I mean, you've spent a lot of hours working on my behalf and I don't really get your investment into this," Ben said coyly.

After buttering a piece of bread and placing it back on his dish, Paul nodded his head, sat back and reflected a moment. "I understand your curiosity, Ben, and it would be bugging me too," he replied finally, then paused again.

"I'm not sure how much your brother Carl has told you. About our friendship, how we know each other and all that …"

"Well, to tell the truth he's been pretty vague, but then, that's Carl! He knows so many people but I never really know quite how they fit in…" Ben said.

Paul cocked his head now, squinting slightly. Then he took a deep breath.

"I'm retired now. You know that, right?" Paul asked.

"Yes, Carl told me that much," Ben replied.

"I was in SF – Special Forces – for years. Then, after an injury, chose to work in the Dip Corps – diplomatic corps – as a security officer – rather than retire," Paul went on.

"Okay, I'm with you so far. Is that where you met Carl?" Ben asked.

"Exactly. We were on assignment in the Czech Republic together at the same time. In fact, I was his driver," Paul said. "It was in the late '90s, during the Balkan War when Carl was attached to NATO, he –"

"I'm sorry, what? I thought he was with the State Department …" Ben said.

Paul interrupted, nodding, "he was, but served as a liaison for NATO there. As his driver, I provided his personal security. We got close and I shared with him the circumstances surrounding my daughter's abuse, which had taken place not long before. Her attacker was a relative and it was a very thorny situation, as you can imagine. Well, Carl pulled some strings here. He arranged it so her perp – who was never prosecuted for her attack because the local prosecutor bungled the case – got thrown in prison for an un-related charge. While serving out his ten-year prison term in the state pen, he was killed and my mind is at ease these days. But, I – and Carl knows this – wrestled with so much back then, it ate me up. So, yeah, whatever I can do, absolutely!"

Ben got it now. And totally trusted Paul. The two shared a great lunch – stroganoff for Ben and chicken Kiev for Paul who shared more about his sketchy "Plan B" if it became necessary.

"It's the kind of thing you'd pull in a situation where 'in case of emergency, break glass' arises, ya know?" Paul explained.

"Totally," Ben replied, warming to the man as they toasted one another over splendid Viennese coffee.

As he drove home, Ben reflected for a while on Paul's situation and how Carl had helped him. He never knew Carl had been working with NATO during the Balkan war. He knew he'd been there for a time, issued a bulletproof vest and sent home a photo of him posing on the famous River Miljacka Bridge at Sarajevo where Archduke Ferdinand and his wife were assassinated. "I'm sure he's got a load of secrets up his sleeve," Ben decided, laughing as he thought of his nerdy elder brother. "A real Walter Mitty!"

With that in mind, he dialed Carl on his cellphone. His brother was out but Ben left a voicemail saying he needed to come down and spend some quality time with Carl and his family soon. He didn't know when it would work out for Carl, but he could really use a break from all this and maybe discuss things further and get Carl's insight, as well. Carl was, after all, a shrewd and incredibly wise man.

At 7 a.m. in the frost-blanketed mountains of northern Italy, Alexander met with his two hoped-for allies. To call them friends was a stretch, but the three had a vested interest in protecting the reputations of both the Pope and the Church as they met over coffee. Their meeting was secret, its contents not to be shared with anyone including other visiting Cardinals and assistants. The air was thick and speech was awkward and strained.

"I have failed utterly!" said the Pope.

"That remains to be seen, Your Eminence," replied Cardinal Ramsey.

"There is still time to salvage things, Your Holiness. Remember the serious troubles faced by your immediate predecessor? We must wait until all the facts are in," stated Cardinal Bertolucci.

"This person making the claim … Clancy? What are we to make of him and what are we to do about him? We can't have him running around threatening blackmail while I am a prisoner here and in Rome." The Pope swallowed hard.

"Shall we excommunicate him?" Ramsey asked.

Alexander adamantly shook his head no.

"From what I understand he left the Church years ago and practices some Eastern religion, Buddhism, if I'm not mistaken," Alexander said. "Excommunication would never work. Right now we simply need to make him a speedy offer that he'll find impossible to refuse. The intelligence shows he maintains ties to his ex-wife and a son. Surely his family would find it worth his while to accept such a large sum? Approach his attorney with $25,000,000, even though he countered with $100 million, adding the standard confidentiality clause. One thing for certain is that we are running out of time!" The Pope was stressing the extreme urgency of the affair, but it was hardly necessary. The meeting went on for another 45 minutes with only a glimmer of a plan.

Cardinals Ramsey and Bertolucci took their leave of the Pope confident of absolutely nothing. They walked in silence until they reached the outer gardens. Though clerics and men of the cloth first, both Ramsey and Bertolucci were realists too, and Alexander chose them as his confidants for a reason. He knew that neither one of them would hesitate to do whatever was necessary to protect him – or rather the church. *Whatever* was necessary. They halted by the olive grove where Bertolucci turned and peered right into his colleague's eyes. "*We* must take care of the problem," he said emphatically.

"We have to give it a little more time," Ramsey pleaded with him, realizing what Bertolucci was suggesting. "Let's see if this Clancy accepts the proposal. Then we can explore other options, don't you think?"

"I suppose that's best," Bertolucci said and shrugged. "In the meantime I have some things to sort out on an unrelated matter, so I'll take my leave if you don't mind."

Ramsey nodded and both men parted and went their separate ways. The Pope and his entourage left for Rome on the following day, but before they did, he summoned Ramsey and Bertolucci to his private chambers for one last secret meeting. The cardinals explained to Alexander that they were formulating a backup plan in the event a monetary settlement wasn't accepted.

"We will not bother you with the details, Your Eminence," Bertolucci said, shooting a stern glance at Ramsey who was about to expand on the comment. Ramsey got the unspoken message and contained himself. Later, when the two were alone together again in the gardens, Bertolucci explained to Ramsey that the Pope had to have plausible deniability, if action was taken, and Bertolucci wasn't sure Ramsey realized that.

The weekend dragged on with no response from the U.S. defense team. Early Monday morning, Cardinal Ramsey and Cardinal Bertolucci met in the open air of St. Peter's Square to review the situation. They agreed to a plan that would be put into motion if this final offer was rejected. The defense team was making one last attempt at a settlement, even trying to approach Ben's ex-wife and son to persuade him to accept the offer. If Clancy didn't accept it, the two Cardinals had no choice, as they saw it, but to unleash whatever they could in one final push to shut this guy up forever.

To better know their adversary, Cardinal Ramsey flew back to his home base – Washington, D.C., Monday afternoon, and on Tuesday set about reviewing the intelligence dossier put together by the Jesuits who had e-mailed it to him at his request. They covered Ben Clancy's history back to Grammar School and he scoured the file in case there was a family member, friend or priest who stood out as a friend or mentor. His hope was to find someone to influence Clancy to accept the very, very generous settlement they were now offering.

Camacho had put his entire staff of 6 priests and 2 nuns to the task of researching the mystery of Ben Clancy and his history. From the St. Adolphus High School archives, the team discovered that Ben's primary education was obtained at Immaculate Heart of Mary School in Wayne, New Jersey. Nothing of note in those files except that Ben had been an exemplary student, and the Monsignor, long dead now, had tried to encourage the Clancy family to put Ben on the path toward the priesthood. A note in the file said that the young protégé's father had bordered on rudeness when he rejected the Monsignor's recommendation.

They learned about Ben's marksmanship skills and his regular attendance at a summer camp run by the Benedictines in Newton, New Jersey. He went there for several years and left abruptly the year he became a Junior Counselor. Interestingly, this was the summer following his alleged molestation by Alexander. Ben was actually close to two counselors there -- one of whom had dropped off the radar entirely. The other was now head priest at a parish in the South Bronx, Monsignor Patrick O'Laughlin. Cardinal Ramsey called the unsuspecting Monsignor that mid-April Tuesday afternoon around 4:30 p.m. O'Laughlin's secretary answered and took a message from the Cardinal, stating that her boss would get back to the esteemed prelate as soon as possible. The Cardinal had very little clue as to where he was going with this, but figured it might be worth a shot. He continued to review the thick dossier on Ben's life with intensity, but all he found on paper was a hard-working man who never quite fulfilled other's expectations of him, but rather stayed under the radar and kept out of trouble for the past several decades.

At around 7:00 p.m., the Bronx Prelate, Monsignor O'Laughlin, called Cardinal Ramsey on his cellphone. Ramsey was eating dinner and excused himself from the table where he was joined by a few of the Archdiocese's upper echelon. He took the call in his private study.

"I would like you to come to my office as soon as possible", the Cardinal said, "Tomorrow would not be too soon. This is an urgent matter for our Mother Church and you may be able to help resolve the issue."

"I see", said the Clergyman, curious as to what the Cardinal had in mind.

"Do you recall a man named Ben Clancy from your time at Camp St. Benedict?" the Cardinal asked.

"Sure! The Clancy's were a good, faithful family," O'Laughlin said. "I was Ben's counselor at summer camp, and Ben was a great kid until --."

"Yes?" Ramsey said, leading.

"Yes, Your Eminence, he was a very good and pious youth, but something changed dramatically when he hit his early teens." The Monsignor recalled. "Is he alright? Gee, I'm afraid I'm lost to --"

"Come and see me tomorrow – please, it's most urgent," the Cardinal ordered, cutting off O'Laughlin mid-sentence.

O'Laughlin could only begin to wonder what this was about as he boarded a train from Grand Central at 6:30 a.m. It was nice to relax to the rocking motion of the train after the busy morning he'd already had -- saying a quick mass at his rectory and arranging for his staff to cancel all of his appointments for the day. He arrived in D.C. around noon. He was used to operating in this manner. His brother worked for the Justice Department and his life was no more clandestine than the Monsignor's. Because of his parish's location, he occasionally received calls in the middle of the night to hear the confession of a dying mobster. Other times he had to play confidante to unwed pregnant teenage girls, ambitious politicians and the occasional businessman. Regardless, he liked his job, it paid well and there was never a dull moment. The "vocation" and calling of his post had long ago worn off as he saw more and more corruption and deception within the ranks of the Church's hierarchy. No longer was he the starry-eyed acolyte out to save the world one soul at a time. Pragmatism had taken hold and he'd love to rise in status and position. Perhaps this was his chance, he thought, forgetting all about the mysterious delving into his time as counselor to Ben Clancy.

When he arrived at the Cardinal's residence, he was greeted by the housekeeper. She showed him to Ramsey's study where His Grace was on the phone. When the high-ranking Cardinal got off the phone he turned and offered the younger priest his ring to kiss. The Monsignor was used to such formalities as this, and it, along with the overtly rich garnerings of the Cardinal's palatial surroundings did not phase him at all. He had signed on with Mother Church and years ago learned to squelch the feeling of unease he had over the wasteful opulence at the expense of the less fortunate. He didn't have to like it, just tolerate it.

Formalities over, the Cardinal bade him to sit. Once Patrick did, Ramsey leaned forward and said in a hushed voice: "Monsignor, we are in very grave trouble."

O'Laughlin raised his eyes to the Cardinals' and saw the fear and concern there. It caught Patrick's attention as much as Ramsey's words did and he listened attentively.

"How well do you know this Ben Clancy, Monsignor?"

"Well, Your Eminence, I haven't seen him in years, and I'm afraid we lost touch completely." O'Laughlin meekly answered.

"He -- Ben Clancy -- has some information that could be greatly damaging to the Pope, Patrick." Seeing the Bronx Pastor's confusion, Ramsey went on. "He has brought about a suit alleging the Pope sexually molested him as a youth and we must do whatever it takes to prevent this from happening," Ramsey said. "Can we count on you?"

Patrick sat back in his chair, looked away from the Cardinal for a moment and quickly thought back to that last summer the younger Clancy was at his beloved camp. Ben never said a word to him, never confided in him, but still, a frown crossed the priest's face as he put things together. The Pope – then Mayron – was Clancy's headmaster at St. Adolphus. Clancy never went back to that school and his behavior changed radically right at the moment he dropped out. Surely there was something that precipitated that. But again, Ben never said a word. But, how could he, Patrick wondered? Poor kid, he must have been filled with shame. And probably a sense of complete betrayal as well, if it were true. It did explain his radical change of behavior though... Still, O'Laughlin was in line to become a Bishop in the not too distant future... He would have to weigh his actions very, very carefully here.

"Monsignor? We'd like to believe we can count on you to help?" Ramsey said testily, breaking into Patrick's thoughts.

"O – of course you can Your Eminence," O'Laughlin answered, finally meeting his superior's eyes again.

"Did you know his family?" The Cardinal probed further.

"Yes, I did. I even stayed with them several times when Ben was in High School. They were a great family, treated me like one of their own, you might say." Patrick said, recalling the large family with the deeply devout parents.

"Did you, you know, have occasion to be physically close to this Ben yourself when he was under your care?" The Cardinal was reaching, but in the wrong direction. Right now, he desperately needed a friend, not an enemy.

"Absolutely not!" exclaimed an indignant O'Laughlin. "I cared for the youth and for his whole family, but not in any inappropriate way ... What are you asking?"

Cardinal Ramsey then cleared his throat and started. "What I am about to tell you is not to leave these chambers, you understand?"

O'Laughlin nodded.

"We are aware that our new Pope, Alexander IX, Cardinal James Mayron, who was your superior in New York City, actually raped and sodomized Ben Clancy in his freshman year at St. Adolphus High School, and that he, Mayron, then expelled the young boy without just cause," Ramsey said, shamefaced and distressed.

O'Laughlin sank back in his chair, stunned. This confirmed his suspicions but would still take a while to digest. Unfortunately, he didn't have that now. His first thought was "Poor Ben!" But realizing his actions were critical to his future in the Church, he pushed that thought out of his mind as the Cardinal spoke on.

"What we are asking you to do is to have a talk with him as soon as possible and convince him to settle with the Church. We are offering him $25,000,000 – 25 *Million*" Ramsey stressed, "and have stipulated that he must be silent on the matter, but I am afraid he steadfastly refuses to comply."

O'Laughlin shrugged, deeply troubled.

"See what you can do to negotiate this thorny situation for us, Patrick. I don't believe threats of excommunication will do any good, but see if you can find some way to reach him and encourage him to accept our generous settlement offer," Ramsey said.

"Well, Your Grace, I'm not sure I ..." O'Laughlin started.

"Monsignor, we do not have much time left before this leaks to the press, in which case *all* our jobs will be in jeopardy!" Ramsey snapped, cutting him off. The Cardinal's whole demeanor had changed. "This is right from His Holiness," he exclaimed, a vein noticeably bulging at his temple.

"I'll see what I can do, Your Eminence," O'Laughlin said, standing. He wanted to probe further, ask if there would be any consequences for the Pope, but it wasn't his position to do so. Ramsey stood and turned his back on the Monsignor, clearly shutting the door on any further dialogue on the matter.

"Report back to me as quickly as possible. Now go," the Cardinal said and waved in dismissal as O'Laughlin took his leave.

A deeply troubled Monsignor O'Laughlin stared out the darkened windows of the black Cadillac Ramsey had dispatched to drive him to Union Station in D.C. where he boarded the next train to New York. All the way back, he reflected on this situation that he had been thrust into. He hadn't seen or heard from Ben Clancy in almost 40 years and he knew that Ben would know the reason for his attempting to contact him. Though his ultimate loyalty was to the Church and to his own ambitions, he had a fondness for the Clancy family, especially Ben. If he could find a way to broker an agreement so everyone came out alive, so to speak, all the better. This was one of those rare moments he regretted his vows and questioned his choice of vocation. The young Ben he knew had so much – the world – going for him. He could've become a Fortune 500 CEO, or, at the very least, made some great contribution to society and/or history. After all, St. Adolphus was known for the prestigious alumni it churned out each year, from famous writers, artists, and CEO's to college presidents, judges, and lawmakers. When Patrick knew Ben, the youth had that kind of potential, the Monsignor recalled.

While in his office, the Cardinal had given O'Laughlin a redacted copy of the file with all the pertinent information he needed regarding the law suit, along with Ben's phone number and address. O'Laughlin's file didn't include the names or contact information of the other victims, however, and he was unaware of them. How he was to approach Ben was entirely up to him. He had several hours to ponder exactly what to do. His instinct told him that Ben would not respond well to a threat of any kind. He arrived back at Grand Central Station several hours later and took a cab back to his rectory in the Bronx.

After a dinner meeting with his subordinates, Monsignor O'Laughlin went to his private quarters and poured himself a drink. He was trembling slightly, fearful of what could happen if he failed. Nonetheless, he dialed Ben's number and waited for someone to pick up. No one answered, and he took it as a sign that a personal visit was the best way to approach it.

O'Laughlin went to bed setting his alarm for 5 a.m. He'd arranged for a driver to take him to Ben's address in Connecticut in the morning and was scanning the file as the Cadillac drove north on the Saw Mill River Parkway toward Interstate 84. The winding roadway made it difficult to read and he closed the file and lay his head back on the headrest, considering what he'd say to Ben.

Chapter 18
Key Strategy

Ben awoke at 8 a.m. and cleared his head with coffee and meditation. He was reading e-mails when a knock at the door startled him out of his reverie. He looked through the peephole to see a middle-aged man and decided it must be a new neighbor.

As he opened the door, he caught a glimpse of a white collar band around a black-shirted neck and regretted it. The voice, though, took him by surprise and he recognized it as that of his old and beloved camp counselor, Patrick O'Laughlin.

"Father Pat!" Ben said, shaking his head with a slight smile as he recalled the pleasant innocent days at camp so many decades ago.

"Monsignor Pat, now," the aging cleric said, smiling fondly at Ben.

Ben's face grew somber now, realizing this meeting was no concidence. Monsignor took note, nodding his head.

"That's right, they've asked me to come," he said. "Look, Ben, I heard what happened to you and I'm so deeply saddened and shocked."

The cleric reached out to touch Ben's arm. Ben stepped backward.

"I only just learned of it, and after I did, I realized the change in your demeanor that last summer – I wish you had come to me, Ben..." O'Laughlin said gently.

"Oh, right! What could I say? I was just banged by that faggot boss of yours? No thanks!" Ben spat out. "I was violated – physically and mentally, and it ruined my life!" O'Laughlin let him continue to vent. "I, I" Ben had to stop now.

"Uhm," the Monsignor acknowledged Ben's point. "Well, I don't know at all what to say other than that I am deeply, deeply sorry, Ben."

Ben inhaled, not sure what he should say. Instead, he remained silent.

Monsignor O'Laughlin was not usually in the uncomfortable position of looking for words, but he had to make a stab at it.

"Look Ben, let's make this right now, then, okay?" the Monsignor said, sensing an opportunity. It was clear to him that Ben was exhausted, emotionally at least, from this battle. "God knows this is weighing you down. If we find a way to resolve it, you can go on with your life."

Ben was tempted and raised his eyes to look deeply into his old friend's. Reliving the abuse was indeed weighing him down. Accepting the settlement would mean he and Jamie and Brad would be able to live in comfort for the rest of their lives... But then, he thought of RAVOC and its leaders and their abuse. And the hundreds of thousands of other victims around the world who had been assaulted by priests and nuns as well..

"It is weighing me down, Pat, but the problem is far bigger than just me. How can all of the other victims get resolution if I sell out now?" Ben asked with honesty and sincerity. Ramsey had been smart to send O'Laughlin, he was definitely the one that might reason with Ben – if anyone could.

"Let's think on this, Ben. Can I – can we sit down?" the Monsignor asked. Ben nodded but remained standing. O'Laughlin was calling upon all of his training now, in an attempt to bring Ben back to his pre-abuse days when the two would engage in Socratic-style discourse. "Sit, Ben, come on…" he said, gesturing toward Ben's recliner.

As much as Ben wanted to fall back into that comfortable pattern, the aging, wiser part of him resisted and he stood, arms crossed, towering above the black-robed cleric.

"I'm comfortable, thanks," Ben answered. "Look, you have no idea what kind of hell was visited upon me by that – despicable Pope of yours."

"Well, yes, I know… I read your file, Ben," it was the priest's turn to interrupt now. "And I am sure there is no apology strong enough, no action harsh enough to make up for what you suffered and endured all these years."

Ben was silent and felt his eyes sting and his throat close up. All he could do was nod in silence.

"But really, Ben, I want you to ask yourself: is holding on to all that going to make up for it? Look, they are offering you a very substantial sum, Ben… Just take it now, and make a good life for yourself, huh?"

Ben frowned and studied his former friend and mentor. And did take a seat now, willing himself to engage … to try to find the way out of this mess.

"But Pat, it's not just about me, don't you see?" Ben explained and implored at the same time.

O'Laughlin smiled and shook his head.

"Absolutely! And I would expect nothing less from you, Ben." Patrick answered. "Look, you think even if you hold out that you can make him accountable? He's -- he will be forced to step down, and will be an outcast for bringing such shame and distrust into the papacy. His legacy will be so dark and dire he'll suffer until the end of his days, trust me."

Ben started to interrupt but O'Laughlin held up his hand to halt him.

"Take the money, Ben, and establish a fund to help others who've been victimized, if that is where your heart leads you. But trust me, no good will come from your continued stubbornness. Even if you let the information go public, your own name and your family's too, will forever be linked with this egregious episode in the Church's history."

Ben nodded, hearing the grain of truth in O'Laughlin's argument. After a moment, he stood, offering a hand to his former mentor.

"It was good to see you again, Pat. Now, if you don't mind, I have some things I need to do," Ben said, escorting the Monsignor to the door.

Flustered, O'Laughlin halted at the doorway.

"Will you at least give it some thought before coming to a decision, Ben? Promise me you'll at least weigh it all out, okay?" The monsignor said as he was exiting the apartment.

"Oh, I will, you can be sure of that, Pat," Ben said. "You've made a strong argument and I really have to reflect on this, but ultimately, the decision is mine and mine alone," he said. O'Laughlin nodded and turned and Ben closed the door behind the cleric.

When he was sure O'Laughlin had driven off, Ben went for a short walk. He thought about what his former friend had said. He had no allegiance to him, and every reason to feel mistrustful. Still, O'Laughlin made some valid points and Ben opted to wait, contact his trusted allies, and reflect more deeply before deciding exactly what to do.

Ben put in a call to Carl to bounce things off him but his brother was out of the country on business and unable to return his call. Reflexively, Ben reached out to Kelly. They had always been close and she had faith in Ben's judgment most of the time, but they had the kind of relationship where, if she felt he was off track, she could say so without hurting his feelings. Kelly's husband genuinely liked Ben too, and believed that even though he had been handed a raw deal in life, he would rebound and ultimately succeed. Ben did not have to choose his words carefully with Kelly. Anything that was on his mind, he could air, as could she. This time, however, the conversation was very specific. After Ben filled Kelly in on his case, he told her about the meeting with Monsignor O'Laughlin earlier that day. He asked her what she thought of it and sought her advice on whether or not he should cave and accept the offer, now at $25 million, which would mean a hefty $15 million after attorney's fees.

"Well, let's look at it from all angles, Ben" Kelly suggested. "On the one hand, that kind of money could set you up for life, and allow you to establish a real legacy for yourself, you know? You'd be crazy not to agree to it."

"Right," Ben said.

"On the other hand, since we are looking at this from both sides, in return for the money, they expect your silence. Others can and probably will continue to be victimized. I don't know, Ben, it's a tough call, and I can't tell you what you should do because you're the one who'll have to live with whatever decision you make."

"I know, Kel, that's why I wanted to get your feedback," Ben replied. "I want to be very clear in my actions, and never second guess what I end up deciding, you know?"

"Absolutely!" Kelly said. "Let me ask you, do you HAVE to make a decision on the settlement right away?"

"N-no, I don't think so," Ben said.

"Well, then, you don't owe these bastards a thing. Let them sweat!" Her emphatic coaching fed into what he, himself, was thinking. "But on the other hand, I'm glad you met with Father Pat. Okay, so he has never bothered to look us up after Mom died, but still, he was a good friend back then and ... well, maybe he's got a saner head in this than some of them in the Vatican, you know?"

"You might be right, Kel. Thanks as always..." Ben said. After a few more minutes discussing the book, Kelly's latest painting, her husband, their kids and the two dogs, Ben said goodbye and promised to keep her posted on any new developments.

After disconnecting from Kelly, Ben called Attorney Sanders, but was unable to reach him and he left an urgent message with the office administrator. He wanted to fill the attorney in on O'Laughlin's visit.

On the ride back to the Bronx, Monsignor O'Laughlin phoned Cardinal Ramsey but his superior was unavailable. O'Laughlin simply left a message that he would call him later.

As ambitious as he was – as a Monsignor, he was literally next in line to become a Bishop in a diocese on Long Island – he still felt a pull of loyalty toward Ben and disgust for what the Pope had done to the youth back then. He recalled the Ben he once knew -- successful at anything he put his mind to, so handsome and personable that he had parts in a handful of television commercials shot in the suburbs that he used to earn his first car. He was on a path to do something great and have a wonderful, outstanding life. The Ben Clancy he remembered had the world in his hands.

The Monsignor then recalled his change of demeanor after his second year of high school and realized Mayron's assault had literally sapped the life out of the young teen. So Pat was torn. Part of him regretted getting drawn into this drama and the ensuing mess that would surely come from this incident and hoped Ben would take the money and go away quietly.

The deeper, more idealistic part of him, though, hoped that Ben *would* call out the Pope. O'Laughlin had served under Alexander when he was Cardinal, and knew him to be a power-hungry, unholy, prick. Yes, in a way, O'Laughlin would love to see Ben publicly shame the Pope and the Church for its despicable behavior in this matter. He had never been on board with the secrecy aspect of the Church's Hierarchy and felt full disclosure and transparency were the best ways to flush out the twisted predators and save the Church. What's more, he thought, who better to do this than the former golden child. Deep down, he really hoped Ben would take up the fight. If things were different, "Father Pat" would have been right there with him every step of the way, fighting that good fight! As it was, unfortunately, he'd have to remain on the sidelines and watch from afar.

Sanders returned Ben's call at around 2 that afternoon. He had been in court all morning on an unrelated matter, he explained. When Ben filled the lawyer in on O'Laughlin's visit, Sanders asked a few questions and quickly formulated a twofold strategy to address the unannounced visit, which he shared with Ben. First, he would contact Camacho at Jesuit Headquarters and warn him to stay away from his client, something he took care of immediately after finishing up with

Ben. Foremost in his mind now though, was concern for his client's safety and the second step revolved around that worry. He gave Ben the name and number of an F.B.I. agent in the New York City area who worked with both Interpol and the Italian Government in investigations regarding the Vatican Bank and international money laundering. The agent's name was Will Thomas and Sanders felt he needed to be made aware of Ben, his situation, and the lawsuit at this point.

"He can advise you on precautions you might want to take until this whole thing is resolved," Sanders explained.

"Precautions?" Ben asked, slightly afraid of the attorney's answer.

"Well," Sanders hesitated, choosing the right words. "The Vatican has a very long reach, as you know. And there have been notable cases of – intimidation – on their part, to ensure they get the desired outcome."

"I get what you are trying to say and while I am not eager for it, I can promise you they will not succeed," Ben said. "In fact, I'm a step ahead and have taken precautions in case anything were to happen to me..."

"I don't think it would ever go that far, Ben, but I am glad you are fully cognizant of all the risks involved," Sanders responded.

Ben thanked the lawyer and said that he would contact Will Thomas as soon as he felt it necessary. He knew that from here on in, perhaps for the remainder of his life, he needed to be extremely careful and vigilant. He was a lone soldier in a religious war that spanned centuries, and he realized if he chose not to settle, he had to be willing to give up his very life if need be so that the truth may finally be heard. He had still not made up his mind on whether to accept or decline the offer, but he knew he could count on his family as well as the leaders within RAVOC to come through if any harm ever did come to him.

His cell phone rang, interrupting his thoughts. It was Carl, who'd returned from his trip overseas and was at the airport.

"Is everything all right?" Carl asked. "I figured if it was important, you'd have left a message with Mia." Mia, Carl's wife of 21 years, was a stunning French beauty Carl met while serving in Paris. They had two great teenage sons, and as a schoolteacher and wife to a diplomat, Mia was kept very busy. Of course Ben would have reached out to her if the matter were pressing.

"Yes, absolutely. Listen, I met with Paul the other day and I would love to come down and spend some time with you guys if you are up to the company?" Ben said, hoping Carl would agree. "I thought I could update you on things and run by you what Paul and I are considering if things fall through."

"Sure, Ben! In fact, I don't know what your plans are but we were hoping to catch *Carmina Burana* -- the Philadelphia Philharmonic's putting it on next weekend if you want to come down and join us?"

"I'd love to and this is perfect timing, I think," Ben replied. "Sitting here waiting for this whole thing to play out is driving me totally nuts, ya know?"

"Great, we'll talk later in the week and figure things out, OK? Do you want to fly? I have extra miles and can get you a ticket if you'd like?" Carl offered.

Ben closed his eyes momentarily, wishing his life were different and he were the one able to be magnanimous. "That's okay, Carl, I think I'll just drive. The weather's turning nice and I love road trips – good chance to think, ya know?"

"Ya sure?" Carl fired back. "OK then, let's talk, say ... midweek and we'll make some plans! Great!"

Ben had opted to join Brad at Jamie's home for dinner that night. He was eager to share with them his visit with Father Pat and would tell them about his planned trip to Philadelphia the next weekend. He expected it would be a pleasant evening with Jamie's typical great food and the three of them sharing a good time. He didn't realize just how wrong he was.

"Why didn't you tell me about that offer," Jamie asked as soon as he took off his jacket. Her agitated expression and aggressive setting of the table clued him in to her mental state.

"What? Oh, well, I planned to tonight, you know, thought we could all discuss it together," Ben answered going toward her to give her a kiss. She brushed past him, turning her cheek away and busied herself with a pot on the stove.

"Take a seat, I'll bring it right out," she said, dismissing him.

"Where's Brad?" Ben asked, noticing his son wasn't there.

"Something came up," she answered curtly.

Ben sat alone somewhat uncomfortably at the dinner table as Jamie fussed in the kitchen for another few minutes. Finally, she came out bearing a large pot of jap chae she placed on a trivet already laid out on the plainly set table.

She took her seat across from Ben and hesitated.

"Let's not discuss it until after dinner, okay?" she said.

"Fine," Ben said, digging into and serving them both hearty portions of the enjoyable dish.

After a silent, uncomfortable dinner, Jamie got up to clear the table. Ben grabbed her hand.

"Hold on," he said. "I sense some serious tension and want to discuss it if you wouldn't mind."

"But I really need to put this away," she answered, breaking away again. She turned and started toward the kitchen, pot in hand.

Ben began clearing dishes as well.

"Leave that, I'll take care of it, you are company," she commanded.

He rolled his eyes. "I'll help, that way we can get it done quicker," he answered, carrying in several stacked plates.

The two maneuvered uncomfortably through the kitchen until finally, the cleaning up was done.

"Now, will you please come and talk to me?" Ben asked.

"Okay," she said, and silently walked toward the sofa following Ben. She sat across from him in an armchair and sighed.

"I have no right to care about what you decide, but I think you are foolish and very hurtful to our son if you reject the offer," she said.

Ben frowned. This had come out of nowhere, really. He thought they were all on the same page and he had gotten the impression both Brad and Jamie were all for his seeking justice. Besides, he had not definitively rejected the offer!

"Where'd you hear I rejected it?" he said, growing visibly upset. Not at her, but at the situation. Things had been going well between them and somehow she was getting information about the settlement and it pissed him off a great deal.

She hesitated and drew a breath.

"Someone from the Jesuits came to see me the other day," she answered. "As I was leaving work."

Ben frowned deeply. More than just angry, now he was starting to get worried. They really had a handle on his life, on the things that were important to him. Were they trying to send a signal? If he didn't accept, what would they do to the ones he loved? He hoped he was exaggerating, but this ticked him off no end. They were getting way too close for comfort. But then, he should have expected this and more.

"That's why Brad didn't come. He won't say it, but he can't help but think you are cheating – yourself and him – out of a good and comfortable life by not accepting this offer, Ben," she said. "It's none of my business what you choose for your life, but as his mother, I agree. I mean, you could provide a very comfortable life for yourself – and him..."

Ben took in her words without saying much at all. He'd been thinking about and looking at this solely from his own point of view when it was clearly going to have implications for them as well. Jamie gallantly took herself out of the equation, but he knew whatever he ended up deciding, she would be included in any material gains made, whether she realized it or not. And he had to consider them both when making up his mind. And of course, Brad as well.

Chapter 19
A Powerful Reality

O'Laughlin measured his words when he followed up with Cardinal Ramsey later that afternoon. Though he tried to phone him from the car, the delay was helpful since he had time to gather his thoughts until he could figure out how this would play out. He felt certain the Pope was behind this effort to secure Ben's silence and it wouldn't hurt Alexander to reflect on the egregious nature of what he'd done. And Ramsey helping him cover this up, well, it showed he was no better! Their acts summed up why Pat had grown so apathetic about his vocation. Shame, he thought, reflecting on the desire he'd had in his younger years to help others and change the world.

"No luck," he said, when he phoned Ramsey back that afternoon. "I did all I could to change his mind and I just get the impression he will not budge."

183

O'Laughlin had decided to really make them squirm. It wasn't a lie, really, since Ben had not agreed to take the settlement right then. And it was anyone's guess what Ben would decide in the end. With RAVOC's influence, he might well decide to keep up his battle anyway.

"Tragic," Ramsey said.

"Well, you can't blame the fellow for having principles," O'Laughlin fired back.

"All right then, well, thank you for trying, Patrick," Ramsey said and disconnected.

After getting the disappointing news from O'Laughlin, Cardinal Ramsey dialed his colleague, Cardinal Bertolucci, in Italy. It was about 9 p.m. there and he knew his colleague would still be up. Bertolucci answered after two short rings. He had been sitting in his study, pondering the situation since well before dinner time and was awaiting this call.

"Good news or bad?" he asked.

"Bad I'm afraid, Clancy won't bite on the settlement. O'Laughlin did persuade him to delay any action for at least a short time, but it looks like he's going to reject the offer. I fear he may be tougher than we had guessed." Ramsey said. "He is in a position to bring the Pope down, and with him all of us I fear, given the current negative perception of the Church."

"I will see what I can do from here," Bertolucci said, frowning deeply.

"Please hurry, my brother! Although O'Laughlin thinks he has bought us time, I am sure the organization, what's its name, RAVOC will continue to keep up their pressure and encourage the idiot to continue his fight." Ramsey answered anxiously.

When they hung up, Cardinal Bertolucci immediately phoned Federico Vitale, a very well-connected businessman from Sicily. The two men were distant cousins and, both having risen through the ranks of Italy's social strata, became closer as the years progressed. His connections, of course, included several "fixers," and Bertolucci knew this well. The high-ranking prelate was able to perform favors for Vitale in the past regarding confession and penance, special masses and more. Hell, he even performed the marriage of Vitale's daughter eight years ago, to a divorcee no less, in a special service at the Cathedral of Monreale which was built in the 1100s by King William II. In return, Vitale cleared the way for Bertolucci in several sensitive situations regarding financial transactions with certain offshore banks in a manner as to give plausible deniability to the Cardinal.

When Vitale heard from his old ally, he was already planning a trip north and agreed to meet in Rome with Bertolucci. As usual, the high ranking Cardinal did not say much over the phone lines, sure that some law enforcement officials were listening – be it the Americans, Scotland Yard, or Italy's own Guardia di Finanza. He simply asked how Vitale's nephew was doing – a code the two had designated years before which meant he needed to see Vitale as soon as possible.

The cardinal then phoned His Holiness for a private meeting. In no time at all, he was in the Pope's chambers where he urged Alexander not to take any action, despite the American's, meaning Ben Clancy – refusal to accept their last best offer. Bertolucci explained to the Pope that he may have found a way out of the predicament.

By now, Alexander was a mere pawn, a figurehead without any independent power or control. The Vatican Hierarchy treated him as if he were terminally ill, making plans for his imminent succession without including him or consulting him. It was only a matter of time, they all believed, before he would resign and it was clear his only allies were

Bertolucci and Ramsey. Few knew how involved the pair were in the Pope's situation, or had any idea the great lengths they were going to, not out of loyalty for him, but to save the Vatican. As Bertolucci left the Pope's chambers, Alexander remained in his quarters, attended to by a few lone priests and nuns who remained in his anteroom, ready to serve at his beck and call.

"Ever since being elected Pope, he has changed dramatically," Father Bernino, the Pope's loyal manservant thought to himself. Bernino had been with the Pope since his days as Cardinal serving in the role of aid in New York City. He found the Cardinal strict and unyielding when it came to matters of faith and doctrine, but deeply caring towards the less fortunate. However much power he wielded first as Bishop, then as Cardinal, and finally as Pope, Alexander still managed acts of compassion. With his latest trials, however, Bernino noticed Alexander withdrawing further and further into himself and becoming far more detached.

After his meeting with the Pope, Bertolucci returned to his chambers, where he waited, fidgeting incessantly with his rosary beads. He knew that he was about to commit a mortal sin, but also knew he could confess it to Cardinal Ramsey, serve his penance, and receive forgiveness for his sin since he was doing this to save the Vatican, after all. He wasn't at all sure that whatever Vitale put in motion would work, but he knew they had no other choice at this point.

In his chambers with Bach playing in the background, Alexander clutched at his prayer book and prayed that he would survive in his position another day. Bertolucci's visit did nothing to reassure him. His mind wandered, and he imagined the scene if he was forced to step down. It would be ugly, he was sure, and the news media – that bloodsucking evil that fed the world's insatiable hunger for scandal and strife -- would no doubt haunt him to the grave. They would delve deeply into his past to find ALL of his secrets! And his family. They would share in his shame and the incredibly painful scrutiny and that truly bothered him. Thank God his mother had died several years ago, for this would surely have killed her!

Federico Vitale, an astute man, was involved in multiple businesses in Sicily, and Milan, Florence and Rome as well as in the U.S. He also had dealings with the Catholic hierarchy, working with several other Cardinals and Bishops besides Bertolucci. In fact, he had so ingratiated himself to the Church that the Vatican's Secretary of State appointed him to head up a commission seeking funding for African Orphans in Ethiopia and Eritrea. His role there served a dual purpose since he also had a financial stake and served as Chairman of a large construction company that had the Vatican Bank's seal of approval. That company was for all purposes merely a front, a funnel of monies that flowed right to the Vatican Bank. The construction was carried out in a number of countries in both Africa and South America and was a major player in the development activities of both regions, garnering public funding, grant money, and private investment dollars all the while enriching the Vatican which had acquired the properties initially. Vitale was resourceful and cagey in all his dealings and had been rewarded handsomely for his efforts.

Arriving by train at 4 that afternoon, Vitale stopped to light a cigarette before entering the Cardinal's quarters. As grandiose and self-absorbed as he was known to be, Vitale was still a bit jealous of the expansive wealth of Bertolucci's residency. The high arches, the carved mahogany doors, marble flooring and the rich tapestries when one walked in spoke of nothing but wealth and power. This was the cathedral that his grandchild was baptized in and its history meant a great deal to him. He had no idea what the Cardinal was about to discuss, but long ago he learned that power attracted power, and the Church and Bertolucci had been good to him. Called out of the blue on an urgent and discrete matter, he knew he was here to pay back a past debt yet again. Not that he minded, for in turn, he could expect another favor when he needed it.

When they met that evening, the Cardinal offered his ring to Vitale who bent on one knee and kissed it. Bertolucci offered his cousin some brandy, which the underworld kingpin gladly accepted. After catching up on family affairs and the latest Italian political news, the Cardinal got to the point.

"We have a person of interest in the New York City area who is proving, well, quite impossible," Bertolucci said. "I cannot go into the details, but he is causing great distress for His Holiness and the Vatican, and the implications of what he may be able to do are drastic. He presents a grave threat to the entire Catholic Church at a time when we can ill afford it."

Vitale nodded.

"And as you know, the Church has been very good to us both," Bertolucci continued. "Federico, can you take care of this problem for us? Of course, you will be rewarded for it handsomely and discretion will be kept at all costs." The Cardinal was stammering at this point.

"Give me the details and I will see what I can do," the businessman answered calmly, very much in control of the situation. The Cardinal quickly obliged and Vitale took his leave. As he watched the gangster walk away, Bertolucci hung his head in shame. He wondered how it ever got to this point and realized he had absolutely not an ounce of integrity left. He, like so many others in this marble prison, had sold his soul for wealth and power a long time ago and there was no getting it back.

As the pressure was mounting for him to come to a decision about this latest counter-offer, Ben found spending time with Jamie helpful, even after their discussion of the other night. Her serene and calm nature soothed the rough edges brought on by the anxiety of the situation which, at any moment could make or break his life forever. Her pointed questions reminded Ben of what was really at stake for him, personally. He still had not given any indication he would accept the massive settlement, but he was leaning that way at this point. It made sense from a personal point of view and truth is, as Father Pat had noted, he was tired of fighting. Still, he had promised his allies at RAVOC that he would give it a few more days to see if perhaps the Church would break down and change their position on the non-disclosure clause, however that was still very doubtful. For the present, Ben tried not to dwell on it too much, unaware of the storm that was brewing across the Atlantic.

It was late at night when Federico Vitale settled into his townhouse off Rome's fashionable Via Condotti. After kicking of his shoes, pouring a scotch and soda, and settling into his brown leather club chair, Vitale opened a shopping bag, took out a new cellphone, turned it on and dialed the number of an old rival. "Yeah, Donald Madrone, please?" the gruff voice asked commandingly.

"Let me get him for you," was the reply. A moment later, another voice came on the line.

"Yes?"

"Madrone!" Vitale was eager to grab his attention.

"Who is this?" Madrone replied.

"Frank Valentine, from Milan," said Vitale. He knew Madrone would figure it out.

"Long time," said Madrone after a brief pause. "How's Business?"

"Business is good, but I have a rotten tooth that needs to be removed. That is why I am calling," Vitale said.

"I may be able to help," Madrone said in the language of compadres used to phone taps and satellite listening devices.

In vague terms, Vitale filled his New York associate in on the urgency of his request. He explained a courier would be dropping off "his x-rays" to review. Madrone assured his Sicilian affiliate that whatever was required, it would be handled expeditiously and with discretion.

In the early 2000s, the U.N. directed the Vatican to produce a document detailing the progress the Church had made on the issue of children's rights and clergy abuse. This promise by the Vatican to produce a report was never delivered upon. Representatives from numerous countries around the seated tables of the United Nations were beginning to take the matter more seriously. To elevate the issue, Brenda and Dan were in New York to meet with representatives of the U.N. Commission on Human Rights to discuss RAVOC's concerns. The two co-founders arranged to meet with a large number of East Coast RAVOC volunteers, as well as with other similarly dedicated groups, whose purpose was to visit any delegates they could, as they were all bound and determined to gain a hearing from the U.N. When they arrived in the city, Brenda called Ben to see if he could join the group for the meeting. Ben declined, explaining that he was heading out of town for the weekend, but offered her and the group encouragement and asked for updates.

In Brooklyn, a promising young member of Madrone's organization, Julian DiLaurio, was pulled aside and told to meet with the boss. Julian's father had been a reliable deputy to Madrone for years before dying in a questionable automobile accident three years earlier. Madrone took the young aspiring gangster aside and in a low voice, whispered instructions to him, handing him a piece of paper with Ben's photograph and address written across it, along with other information about Ben. Julian's eyes met the older man's; he nodded, whispered something, and put the address into his cellphone. He committed the photo to memory, crumpled it up, and trashed it as he headed out of the freight forwarding offices that served as the Madrone family's official headquarters.

The young soldier then stopped by his own apartment, put a few things together then left in his car, a black Jeep Cherokee. Crossing the Whitestone Bridge and heading up the Hutchinson River Parkway toward Connecticut, he cranked up the radio – playing Vivaldi -- as he drove.

Arriving in Ben's neighborhood, Julian saw that Ben's car, a red Honda Accord, was not there, so he waited. At around 11 p.m., 6 hours later, Ben finally arrived home and went inside. Julian waited three more hours, certain that most residents were asleep. Cloaked in darkness and wearing dark clothing, he casually walked over to Ben's vehicle, dropped something on the ground, made it look like he was picking it up and smoothly and easily affixed something to the undercarriage of Ben's car. Returning to his own car, Julian got in, put it in gear and drove back to New York.

The next day, Ben had a quiet morning and no plans to go anywhere until after lunch, when he had to go to the Post Office. He ate quickly, grabbed the outgoing mail, and was headed to the car when he was stopped by one of the other tenants in front of his building, wanting to discuss a meeting scheduled for the following week. As they talked, he turned towards his car and pushed the remote starter button on the car. A huge explosion knocked him backwards as his car was engulfed in flames. He knew immediately that someone had done this intentionally. He had absolutely no doubt. He also knew that his life had changed forever.

The police arrived within 15 minutes and dispatched the fire department who put out the burning embers of the completely destroyed car. Ben knew Brit Hargrove, the investigating police officer from his time in Alcoholics Anonymous, and mentioned his legal settlement with the Church, pointing to the obvious correlation. Stunned and shaken, Ben begged to leave the scene quickly. After he was questioned, Brit agreed let him go, but called out to him to stop.

"Ben, wait," Brit jogged over toward him and asked softly, "do you think you need more protection?"

"I'm sure!" said Ben only half in jest.

In shock, Ben walked to the local diner where he grabbed a cup of coffee and made several calls. The first was to his auto insurance company, and next he called for a rental car, paying extra for one that offered a remote starter. He then called Jeff, a cousin who had an extensive gun collection. Once the rental car had been delivered, he drove over to his cousin's place in the country. There, Ben filled him in on the situation and asked if he could borrow a hand gun for protection, suggesting Jeff pick it out for him.

Knowing this was bending the law, Jeff still agreed without hesitation, and handed him a nice Sig Sauer .9 mm, along with a carton of ammunition too. As he explained to Ben about the clip, safety, and cleaning requirements, Jeff asked him what else he could do. The two were close growing up, and Jeff knew of Ben's bi-polar disorder. Although that set off some alarm bells when Ben'd first asked for the gun, he knew about Ben's recovery and the two had become good friends in recent years. Jeff was actually best man at Ben's wedding.

"At the very least, I can take you to the shooting range if you want, Ben," Jeff offered.

"We'll see. For now, just keep your eyes open," Ben said. "I really appreciate it, though, Jeff. If all goes to plan, you'll have the gun back in a month or less."

"You wanna stay the night?" Jeff asked as it was getting dark now.

"Nah, I've got tons to do and am heading down to Carl's for the weekend, day after tomorrow," Ben said.

Ben drove the late model Hyundai Sonata rental car over to pay Brad a visit. As he pulled into the driveway, Brad was there to greet him, eying the rental car with curiosity. Ben smiled and shook his head "no."

"No, I didn't settle and no, this isn't my new car," he said simply. They had coffee together and Ben told Brad about the bombing incident.

"Mother Fuckers!" Brad said, greatly upset.

Ben sighed and looked closely at his son.

"We need to talk, Brad," Ben said. "Your opinion means a great deal to me."

Brad shrugged, "Okay, let's do this."

They sat together over refilled coffee mugs discussing Ben's case and the offer in depth. Like his mother, Brad did not want to tell Ben whether to accept the settlement or not. And since the bombing, he'd possibly even changed his mind about it too.

"Part of me hopes you take them all down, Dad," Brad said. "Starting with that asshole that assaulted you, of course."

Ben smiled.

"I appreciate your support, Brad, but that is a huge amount of money we are looking at here," Ben said.

"Yeah, you are, Dad," Brad said, stressing the pronoun.

Ben looked at his wise son and smiled. "You're not gonna give me the answer, are you?" he asked his son.

"I can't Dad. This is on you. Your decision, your life, your money. I can't tell you how to decide on this, sorry!" Brad smiled and gave Ben a playful punch.

"Son of a gun! You're just as maddeningly wise as your mother!" Ben said, punching playfully back. As he did, he noticed the time.

"Oh shit! I've gotta go! I'm due to fly out the day after tomorrow and I've got tons to do!" Ben said.

He reminded Brad to work with Kelly to get the manuscript published by any means possible if anything should happen to him.

"Not that it will, of course," Ben said, with a grin as he walked backwards toward his car. "Are we still on for B-ball Wednesday night?"

Growing serious a moment, though, Ben stopped to stress his next words.

"Just whatever happens, promise me you'll take care of your mother, okay?" Brad started to protest but Ben held up a hand to silence him. "You know, I was never able to get life insurance because of my bi-polar disorder, and I…"

"Dad!" Brad said, cutting him off. "Cut it with the glum thoughts, will ya? This was probably just a freak accident!"

"I'm sure you're right," Ben said. But both knew the truth: someone had placed that bomb under Ben's car hoping to kill him.

"I love you" said Brad walking alongside Ben, "please be careful!"

"I love you, too." Ben answered, looking seriously into his son's eyes.

He then drove home, estimating how much time he had before the next attack. Once they received word that he had not died, a day at the most is what he figured. From his cellphone he called Will Thomas, the FBI agent that Sanders had recommended. The agent was out in the field but would be back later in the day. Ben left a message, stating its importance. He then called Paul who wasn't there either. After this second call, he reached Kelly and filled her in on the morning's incident.

"Fucking bastards!" she shouted into the phone. "They can't accept reality so they steal and cheat and lie and kill to bend the truth to their liking!"

Ben listened, half-smiling. His sister's Irish was up. "*Katie, bar the door!*" he thought to himself. It took a great deal to unsettle Kelly, but when she got pissed, there was nothing stopping her. And he was ever so glad she was on his side in this battle.

"Ben, so help me God, we're going to nail those bastards!"

Ben reminded her that Brad also had a copy of the manuscript and Ben expected her to get it into publication if anything happened. He also told her how he'd gotten a gun from Jeff. Practical and pragmatic, Ben wasn't troubled that she didn't want to waste time with expressions of concern for his well-being which he knew she felt.

"Oh, perfect! Jeff's exactly who you want to go to for that!" Kelly said. She was great at thinking on her feet, his sister, and didn't care at all that his carrying the gun was outside of the law. "You might even ask him if any of his buddies would serve as voluntary security for you for the time being."

"Great idea, Kel, but I don't want to blow this out of proportion yet," he said, "we don't even know for sure it was a bomb."

She wasn't able to persuade him to seek additional protection from Jeff's pals, and they disconnected shortly thereafter. Ben tried the attorney again but he wasn't there so he left him a message. He didn't want to make any calls to RAVOC knowing the leaders were busy with their U.N. lobbying. He drove the remainder of the way home in quiet.

It was dark when he got home, and he checked all the doors and windows to make sure no one had broken in. He took the gun out from behind his waistband and set it down on his dresser. His cellphone rang and it was Paul.

"Paul, perfect timing, my new friend!" Ben said. He proceeded to fill Paul in on the car bombing.

"Of course it was them," Paul said when Ben raised doubts. "They have a huge amount to lose here, Ben. You need to be very careful from this moment on, am I clear?"

Ben told Paul about the gun he'd borrowed.

"Good for you!" Paul said. "But if they're contractors, that won't mean shit, I'm afraid. I think it's time for Plan B, Ben."

"I was thinking the exact same thing, Paul! If I set it in motion, will you be free in the next few days if I need you?"

"Of course, I will," Paul said. "Call me and I'll drop whatever I'm doing, Ben. I got your back on this."

"Thanks man," Ben said. The two disconnected shortly thereafter.

Feeling like he was somewhat in control of an extraordinarily difficult and dangerous situation, he went out onto the porch and played his guitar for a long time, staring up at the warm May evening sky. He was now beginning to envision a future that embraced a far bigger picture.

Jerry Sanders, the attorney, called Ben back a short while later, interrupting his reverie. Ben filled him in on the car bomb incident and told Sanders he was now ready to settle. He also expressed his strongest hope that the settlement could take place within the next 24 hours.

"I won't be able to reach Camacho tonight," Sanders said, looking at his Rolex. "I'll get to him first thing in the morning, though, and tell him to expedite it. We'll see how quickly we can get this done."

"That'd be great," Ben said.

He called Carl after this and told him he might have to delay his trip. "I'll explain in detail when I come but I'll call before I plan anything to make sure you're there," he told his brother.

"Kelly told me a little about what happened…" Carl said, voice expressing concern. "You okay up there?"

"I will be, Carl. Don't worry, I think it's all under control here," Ben replied as his phone clicked, indicating another call was coming through. "Look, I got another call, let me run. Sorry about the change in plans, I'll call you in a day or two, okay?"

"You got it, take care," Carl said, disconnecting.

PART FIVE

The Settlement

Chapter 20
The Settlement

Attorney Sanders left a voice mail for Father Camacho who, as expected, was unavailable. After that, he decided to call Attorney Demarest, the lawyer for the Church and, after reaching him successfully, was assured that the settlement papers would be in hand by 10 a.m. via overnight courier. Sanders immediately called Ben back and asked him to aim for signing off on the legal docs around 2 p.m., and that he would have the New York Office call as soon as the paperwork arrived the next morning, to confirm the planned appointment.

When he hung up, Ben began preparing dinner when the phone rang again. It was Will Thomas from the FBI. Will said that he had familiarized himself with Ben's case and offered to help in any way that he could. Ben told him they were arranging a settlement meeting for the next day, which they both felt would mean Ben would be out of danger. Still, the agent warned Ben to take extra precautions and told him that he would send over a protection detail just to be safe. Ben thanked him and went about his business.

A knock at the door at 8:45 p.m. startled Ben from his reflections. He answered after seeing a law enforcement badge as he looked through the peephole. At the door, an FBI special agent introduced himself and told Ben he was assigned to guard him.

"I'll be down the hallway keeping watch for the night," he said.

"Want some coffee?" Ben asked.

The agent just held up his Dunkin Donuts coffee cup and shook his head.

"All right then. Hey, thanks," Ben said. The agent was already walking away and waved casually over his shoulder.

Ben closed the door feeling reassured and at ease, and thought he might even get some sleep during the night. Just in case, though, when he went to bed, he removed the safety off the handgun he had borrowed from his cousin, set it right by his side on the nightstand and slept fitfully at best. At two in the morning, he heard a scratching sound from the front door. Alert, Ben jumped out of bed, grabbed the 9 mm, and crept silently across the floor to hide behind the bedroom door in the darkness. He listened silently as he heard the front door open and the sound of footsteps approaching the bedroom. A dark-clothed intruder headed toward the bed, hand holding a hypodermic needle. He crept toward the shape in the bed, preparing to inject the needle into the body. As he did, Ben moved from his hiding place to fire several shots into the man's chest, saving several bullets just in case this man was not alone.

Blood escaped the multiple holes in the intruders' body and created a large pool of crimson on the ground where the dead man fell, eyes still open. Neighbors called the police and Brit Hargrove arrived soon after, along with the paramedics. The FBI agent who had pulled guard duty for Ben lay slumped in the stairway, piano wire still entwined around his neck. Hargrove was on the phone to the local FBI office immediately and despite the hour, Ben called Will Thomas to let him know his agent had been killed. Will immediately coordinated with the local office for additional protective custody and told Ben that he'd check in with him in the morning.

A shaken Ben was escorted to and spent the rest of the night in a non-descript room at the local Comfort Suites downtown with two agents in the adjoining room and another in the hallway. At least he was warm and relatively safe, Ben thought, realizing it was only his sharp hearing and quick action that had saved him. Now unable to sleep, he lay there, his jaw set with determination.

Back at Ben's apartment, the killer's fingerprints were scanned into the FBI's database and a search for his identity commenced. Links to the Madrone crime family soon become apparent to the FBI and were related to Thomas. Having lost a good agent, Will Thomas was in no mood to let this pass. Because of the extensive Mafia network living and operating within his jurisdiction, he had been part of a joint task force working with Interpol to identify criminal links between the Vatican, its Bank, and the Mafia. He felt sure these two attacks on Clancy could be traced right back to the Holy See and an Italian businessman who had recently crept up on his radar: Federico Vitale.

Recognizing the relentless determination in the pair of attacks, Thomas remained deeply concerned for Ben's welfare and within a couple of hours, he arranged for Ben to be taken to a safe house in Suffolk County, New York. As they spoke by phone, Ben told the tall, red-haired senior agent of his plans to sign the settlement papers in lower Manhattan at Attorney O'Donnell's office that afternoon. He also mentioned his upcoming trip to see his brother in Philadelphia.   As instructed, Ben handed the telephone to the lead agent in his security detail, Field Agent Danny Jackson.

"Stay with Ben no matter what. That's gonna mean a trip into New York City today and it is likely that the guys behind this know where he'll be, so be especially wary," Will told Jackson. "I already lost one good man, I'm not about to lose any more, you hear?"

"Got it, sir," the agent said and handed the phone back to Ben as instructed.

"Thanks," Ben said. "When this is all over with, I'll owe you bigtime."

"Just do what you gotta, Ben, and good luck!" said the agent.

As instructed, Ben phoned Sanders' New York office at 10 and spoke with O'Donnell. The papers had indeed arrived and the signing was on as scheduled for 2 o'clock Eastern Time.

"I'm looking them over right now, but they appear in order," O'Donnell said. "Unless you hear from me in the next hour, we'll see you then."

After disconnecting, Ben ate a light breakfast and sipped the coffee that one of the members of the security detail brought him from the lobby dining room, then used his cell phone to call Jamie.

After explaining what had happened over the last 24 hours, Ben urged her to spend the night with a friend.

"I'm worried about *ALL* of us! Who knows what they might do," he said. Moving out of earshot from his escort now, he spoke in a softer tone, asking her to understand why he had been inattentive to her needs when they were married.

"No need to explain, Ben, and certainly, now is not the right time for such a discussion," she said, cutting him off.

"You're right," he said, "Listen, I love you, no matter what, okay? Please be careful and make sure that Brad knows what's going on and that he stays with a friend as well."

After saying goodbye to Jamie, Ben called Kelly, told her what had happened during the night and reassured her that he was alright and that he indeed had a plan for all this.

"My God", said Kelly, "This is huge. Ben, please take care of yourself and don't let the agents out of your sight. This will be over soon, thank God! When it is, why don't you plan on staying with Rob and me for a few days while you get your living arrangements sorted out?"

"That'd be nice," said Ben, "but we've got a lot of work to do before then. I gotta go, but I'll call you later this afternoon, okay? Love ya, Kel."

Beth reached him around noon as he was heading out the door for the drive to New York City to update him on their outreach to the U.N. Ben told her that he had something very important to take care of in the afternoon, but that he would call her that night. She was unaware of the attempt on his life the night before and he felt it better to keep it quiet for now. He hoped she wouldn't hear it on the news before he could explain it all.

Cardinal Ramsey who had returned to the Vatican for the week, shared the good news of the impending settlement with Cardinal Bertolucci.

"Well, that's encouraging," Bertolucci said, not bothering Ramsey with the details about the murder attempts. "I'm glad he saw the light. See, everyone has a price. I think perhaps your Monsignor did persuade him after all. Thank God, we may now move forward and put this sordid episode behind us."

It was late that same evening in Milan when Federico Vitale called Cardinal Bertolucci to say that he had failed.

"Essere fottuto!" he exclaimed. "La testa di merda!"

Vitale related to Bertolucci that his "man" had been killed and that he had no confidence in the connection he had assigned this task to.

"Affanculo! I should never have trusted him!" he vented, not giving Bertolucci a chance to speak. Infuriated, he offered to fly a man he trusted to Manhattan himself to take care of the problem, but Bertolucci finally had a chance to speak and told him that it would not be necessary after all.

"The pressure must have been enough to persuade him to sign the papers and today it is to be concluded!" Bertolucci exclaimed. "So your contact did his job well enough after all!"

"I'm glad to hear this Clancy is thinking rationally about his prospects," Vitale said, relieved.

In the safe house, Jackson turned his bulky frame toward Ben who stepped from the restroom.

"Are we ready? Let's head out then!" Jackson said, securing his holster and grabbing his keys.

Ben looked out the sedan's window to the roadsigns on the Long Island Expressway and was pensive and silent. He hoped things would go as he had planned and wondered if he was doing the right thing. Even Will Thomas, though he might have approved, was not privy to Ben's real scheme, and perhaps Ben should have alerted him to his plans...

He continued to second guess himself for a time and soon, Jackson pulled into the parking garage near Attorney O'Donnell's law offices at 1:45. They walked to the front door and went up together. The other security team remained behind in their car, parked down the block from the building entrance.   Jackson almost missed the subtle nod of acknowledgement Ben gave to a tall black man buying coffee at the concession stand in the lobby and wondered briefly what that was all about.   Ben was used to traveling alone, but Jackson proved to be good and, importantly, well-informed company as he had worked with Will Thomas on the Vatican task force.   When they were shown to the conference room, Ben deliberately chose a seat with his back closest to the door though another seat on the other side had been designated for him as it had been the last time they'd all met.

"I'm just a little weird like that," he said sheepishly to Sanders who looked at him quizzically, shrugged, and moved his paperwork to the end of the table nearest Ben. "We can sit the defense on the other side."

When Attorney Demarest cockily strode into the conference room a few minutes later, Ben refused to shake his outstretched hand.   Instead, he ignored the entourage that made up the counsel for the defense as they moved through the room and clumsily took their seats across the table from Ben, and Attorneys Sanders and O'Donnell.

Formalities dispensed with, Ben was fidgeting with his newly purchased Smartphone and all attention turned toward it. Sanders was about to place a paternal hand over the phone, but Ben set it down on his own.   He still hadn't raised his eyes to look at the Church's defense team.

"Before we sign anything, I want to hear it," Ben insisted, still looking down at his new "toy" and refusing to make eye contact across the room.

"Excuse me?" Camacho asked.

"An apology. I think it's only fair, don't you?" Ben said, finally shooting a withering glare across the table.

Camacho and Demarest looked at one another and shrugged. Attorney Demarest, the counsel for the Catholic Church cleared his throat and stood to speak.

"His Holiness, Pope Alexander, is deeply remorseful over the occurrences that have brought us here, but hopes in good faith that this matter can now be resolved."

Sanders then in a businesslike manner reviewed the terms of the settlement and signed his name. He then gave the document over for Demarest to sign.

"It's just all ceremonious bullshit," Ben said aloud with a smirk.

Attorney Demarest eyed him with disdain as he signed the papers. He then passed the document across the table to Ben pointing to where he should sign. Ben sat for a moment and held the paper in front of him.

"I'm sorry, but before I sign my life away, can we review this one more time please?" he said.

Camacho and Demarest looked exasperatedly at Sanders who held up his hand to silence them.

"My client has every right to this," he said.

"In signing this, Ben, you are releasing the Vatican, his Excellency Pope Alexander IX, St. Adolphus High School in New York City, and the New York Archdiocese from any further claim to damages you encountered due to an incident in which you claim Pope Alexander, then the headmaster of St. Adolphus High School, raped and sodomized you." Attorney Sanders pointed to an item on page three of the lengthy document. "See, here is the description in detail of the encounter as you related it during the deposition."

"In return, you will be receiving a sum of $25 million U.S. Actually, I should have explained this more clearly and I apologize," Sanders continued. His attention, though, shifted toward the team of attorneys sitting opposite him.

"Gentlemen, please bear with us only a few more minutes, if you don't mind," he said curtly.

Camacho and Demarest looked down.

"The funds will be transferred into our legal accounts, Ben. We will deduct our 33-1/3 percent for representing you, and then, will transfer the remainder into whatever accounts you designate," he explained to Ben.

"I see," Ben said. "And in effect, this is an admission of guilt by the Pope, right?"

The defense attorneys looked uncomfortably at one another and at Sanders.

"It could be construed as such," Sanders said in his most lawyerly manner. "But essentially…"

"Okay," Ben nodded, cutting him off.

"But that brings up the last and perhaps most important point of this entire settlement and I want to be totally clear with you, Ben," Sanders continued. "By signing this, and by accepting the $25 million, you are accepting the stipulation of confidentiality in this case. This is how it reads, Ben."

O'Donnell, who'd been quiet until now, saw the defense team fidgeting and pre-empted any verbal protests. "Gentlemen, he has had no chance to review this agreement and is seeing it for the first time right now. I would think you could spare the theatrics and be patient, don't you?" he asked.

Camacho and Demarest sank back into their chairs as Sanders continued, showing Ben the document's section where the confidentiality clause was written.

" *To the maximum extent permitted by law, the parties further agree that this Agreement, the terms and conditions of this Agreement, the facts, events and issues which gave rise to this Agreement, and any and all actions by Mr. Ben Clancy and St.*

Adolphus High School, the New York Archdiocese, Pope Alexander IX, and the Roman Catholic Church, based in Vatican City, in accordance therewith, are strictly confidential and shall not be disclosed or discussed with any other persons, entities or organizations, except as may be required by applicable law. "

Ben frowned, took the document from Sanders, folded it, gathered his Smartphone, stood up and walked without a trace of hesitation to the nearby door.

"Where are you going?" Demarest asked, taken aback.

"I'm going to call my mother! I'll only be a minute," Ben replied, moving quickly out of the room.

Agent Jackson who was waiting just outside the conference room, swiftly followed him out to the law firm's lobby, through the entry doors and to a stairwell at the end of the hall. Ben took the steps three at a time and Jackson had to sprint to keep up with him.

Inside the room, the attorneys and staffers, puzzled by Ben's departure, sat for a few moments, then slowly rose to their feet. Sanders was the first to exit the room but his client was already gone.

"Just where are you going?" Jackson asked, confused, but following.

"It's alright, just follow me!" Ben called over his shoulder.

They left the stairwell by a doorway that exited the building onto 14th Street where a Black SUV with dark tinted windows was waiting. Ben opened the passenger's side door but the agent began to draw his weapon.

"It's okay," Ben said, placing his hand on Jackson's arm. "I know what I'm doing."

The agent got into the backseat and activated his cellphone.

"Mind telling me what the fuck we're doing, Ben?" he said, angrily, punching in the number for his boss.

"Well, I did warn you that I had things in motion," Ben said. "I just didn't want to share too much with you for fear you'd, you know…"

Jackson held up a finger as he listened on his cell phone.

"Yeah, can you get back to me? It's okay, but I wanted to update you," he said and disconnected.

"Sorry, hey, this is Paul Adams. Paul, meet Agent Danny Jackson of the FBI."

Paul looked into the rear view mirror and grinned. "Apologies, I've been where you are before and know it's not cool. Ben, explain to Agent Jackson what's about to go down."

"We'll be stopping at a Kinko's on West 40th Street in a minute or so," Ben responded without missing a beat.

"Kinko's?" Jackson asked with curiosity.

Ben nodded.

"You'll see," Ben said. Adrenalin was pumping and Ben's nerves were jagged even though he thought things had gone perfectly in the law offices. Even better than he'd hoped, with Sanders playing an unsuspecting assistant in getting all the information he could possibly want on the record.

"I already sussed out a parking spot earlier," Paul said, turning the car into a lot and pulling the ticket from the automated gate.

The trio left the parked car, Paul in the lead. Ben was handling his Smartphone and Paul turned to look at him.

"You get anything good?" he asked.

"Great stuff," Ben said, smiling as Paul, who was carrying a USB cable, took the phone. Paul plugged the cable into the phone's socket as they entered the Kinko's.

"I need a computer please," Paul said. A clerk pointed to the bank of computers on the far wall and took the credit card from Paul's outstretched hand.

"PC or Mac?" the clerk asked.

"PC," Paul answered and after signing the credit card slip, headed to the bank of computers.

Jackson, somewhat bewildered, remained with Ben who took the legal papers to a copy machine, inserted a credit card and punched in the correct commands to make five copies of the documents at the right size. Finally realizing what was going on, Jackson leaned up against an empty machine, crossed his arms and smiled.

"Okay then!" he said. "I hope one of those is for us?"

"Of course," Ben replied, smiling.

While waiting for the copies, Ben pulled out his old cellphone and called Attorney Sanders.

Sanders' usually cool voice betrayed his confusion and anger.

"What happened, Ben?" He asked.

"Something came up, something I needed to do. I'm sorry to have inconvenienced you but I'll call you in a day or so." Ben then hung up the phone and gazed out on the streets of the city as the photocopy machine buzzed along. He turned his gaze to a computer station where Paul was busy tapping away at the computer keyboard, maneuvering a thumb drive into another USB port, and keying commands into the Smartphone.

Chapter 21
Power Play

After completing their business at Kinko's, the trio walked rapidly up the street three blocks north, to Eighth Ave. between 40th and 41st, entering the headquarters of publishing giant *The New York Times*. By this time, Agent Jackson realized Adams and his client had a game plan all their own and he was clearly along just for the ride. He sensed that Adams had a background in the military or security services and the unanticipated departure from plan was made more tolerable because of it, though he remained alert and careful with regard to his charge. Adams and Ben strode purposefully through the revolving doors with field agent Jackson on their heels. At the front desk, Ben filled out the visitor's log and asked for Hugh Bradley, and looked over to see Paul nod confirmation. Bradley was called and the trio were directed up to the 6th floor. In the elevator, little was said until Paul broke into their thoughts.

"You know how you're gonna approach him?"

"Absolutely," Ben said with confidence in his voice. "I kinda feel like the worst part is behind me," Ben said. "And I can't thank you enough for doing all this background work to set this up," he added, nudging the big man in a friendly way.

Hugh met them at the elevator and shook Ben's hand, then Paul's, and eyed the agent.

"I wasn't sure you'd come, Ben, but I'm glad you did…" Bradley said. "Who's the suit and is his presence really necessary?" asked the reporter.

Quite!" Ben replied. "Believe it or not, I've had a couple of very near misses lately and kinda want to hang around a while longer. He's here to make sure I do."

The Pulitzer-nominated reporter escorted them toward his office near the window, halting at a coffee machine in the break room nearby first. As he indicated the coffee, Ben and Paul accepted and Paul poured them both a cup. Jackson declined courteously.

They entered Bradley's office and sat down as Jackson stood guard outside the doorway. Ben began talking before they even sat down in a hurried, excited manner.

"Slow down Ben, this sounds huge. Lay it out for me."

Ben pulled the settlement agreement from his breast pocket, and the reporter quickly noticed that he had not signed it. "They offered you this?" Bradley asked.

Ben nodded.

"My God" said the reporter, studying the document. After several minutes, he finally spoke, reaching into his desk drawer as he did.

"Do you mind if we get this on tape?" he asked, looking questioningly at Ben and Paul.

Ben said "Absolutely not!" He wanted this story to come out, in its entirety and with complete accuracy. Recording their discussion would ensure that happened.

Bradley flipped a switch on his handheld device and began asking question after question of Ben, who answered deliberately and factually. More than once Bradley shook his head in disbelief and amazement, looking over at Paul who nodded confirmation.

"Do you know what this means?" the reporter asked.

"Absolutely! That's why I am here," Ben said, leaning forward in his chair. "I've read your coverage in the past and I admire your courage. I trust you can work with this information?"

Bradley nodded, cleared his throat, and asked Ben several more questions, including some about his childhood, experiences at other schools, and more. Ben answered each of the follow-up questions without hesitation and at the end of the interview Bradley asked for one more thing: the contact information for the other victims of Mayron.

"I imagine your lawyer has them and can't release them due to confidentiality, but I thought I'd ask. It will be necessary to this story to have independent verification of your allegations and it would also save me a lot of digging if you have that information.

"Of course … I already have that info, Hugh!" Ben said, and pulled out a handwritten list with each identified victim's name and contact information which he handed to Bradley.

Bradley shot a questioning glance at Ben as he looked over the information.

"How'd you?" he asked. "Never mind, I'm sure I don't really want to know, but this is great! Perfect!" Bradley said, placing the paper carefully inside a fresh manila folder on his desk.

All done answering questions, Ben had one for Bradley.

"When do you expect this to go to print?" he asked.

"I've already been in discussion with the editors as to how to present what we planned as an enterprise piece – you know, several articles joined together by the overarching story about you, the Pope, and St. Adolphus," Bradley said. "We'll obviously have to do some fact checking and more digging before we can let it fly, but I'd think we'd aim for the first segment to go in the Sunday paper, which would give us the biggest splash and viewership."

Ben and Paul stood, preparing to leave and Ben looked at Paul before speaking to the *Times* reporter. "One last thing, I want to let you know we've approached the *Washington Post* as well."

"Shit, Ben!" Bradley said running his fingers through his graying hair. "With something this hot, we REALLY need to be sure we've got the facts right!"

"You do," Ben said as the pair exited the room. Over his shoulder, he called back "If it's not in Sunday's paper, we've got a copy of all our material for Aikers at the Post. Just letting you know."

The trio, Ben, Paul and Agent Jackson, left the building and went to a coffee shop on the other side of the Port Authority Bus Terminal for a wrap-up conversation.

"That went extremely well," Paul said. "I'm really impressed with how you handled yourself, Ben! Great job."

"Thanks Paul," Ben replied. "It was your coaching that gave me the confidence to pull it off."

He grew sober then.

"Now what?" Ben asked.

"Good question," Jackson piped in. They'd forgotten all about the agent's presence and both looked over at him.

"Have you notified Thomas?" He asked as Ben and Paul looked at one another. "I intend to, as soon as I can figure out where we're heading with all of this" Jackson said.

After finishing their coffee, they got back into Paul's SUV and drove to the parking lot downtown where Jackson's government issued sedan was waiting. Paul waited for them to get in and safely out of the parking lot and onto Eighth Avenue before turning his car toward Brooklyn Heights where he had a pricey but pleasant townhouse with a stunning view of Manhattan.

Jackson was navigating through the Queens Midtown Tunnel as he checked in with his superior who was still incommunicado, so he left Agent Thomas a voice mail saying he'd call later to fill him in on the day's events. After exiting onto the interstate, Ben put in an ear bud and dialed Carl's number.

"Hey, I'm sorry but I won't be able to make it," he said. "I was not sure but something came up and it's – well, it's for the best, you'll see."

He listened as Carl spoke, and then responded: "Yeah, everything's fine now. But keep watching the news," he said cryptically. "I've gotta go, but take care. Sorry again."

After disconnecting, Ben called Attorney Sanders.

"I realize I owe you an explanation," Ben said. "I'd rather not discuss it over the phone and right now I'm tired and I'm going to get some dinner, a hot shower and some rest. I'll be in touch as soon as I can."

Sanders looked blankly at the telephone instrument for seconds after Ben disconnected. He was still in the conference room with the defense team and had to think fast. He got to his feet, excused himself, called for his partner to join him and the two stepped into Sanders' office, shutting the door behind them.

"What the fuck?" O'Donnell said. "We've been played, haven't we?"

"Looks that way, but he refused to confirm it," Sanders said, secretly pleased that Ben had decided not to cash in. It would mean a huge loss of revenue for the firm, but this was one case he'd rather try in the court of public opinion any day.

Together they walked back into the conference room and with grim faces explained to Camacho and Demarest that it appeared their client was suffering cold feet.

"I'm sure he'll be ready to settle in a day or two," Sanders said, stalling. "It is a tremendous thing he needs to consider, and, in case you are not aware, there was an attempt on his life last night."

"What?" Demarest asked, frowning. This kind of shit wouldn't help at all. He glared at Camacho who shrugged. "I had no idea," he said as the pair stood to take their leave.

"We'll keep you posted when we hear from Ben. As I said, I'm sure he just got cold feet," O'Donnell said, and Ben's team shook hands with the opposing counsel and escorted them out of the offices.

Ben and Jackson pulled off the L.I.E. and got back to the safe house before dusk. Jackson offered Ben a cold soft drink and opened one for himself.

"That took guts," the agent said calmly, admiringly, "I'm impressed with how you both planned this out and yeah ... it definitely took a lot of guts!"

Attorney Demarest was frantic. He and Father Greg Camacho had a long conversation and some sharp words for one another on their ride uptown after waiting for almost three hours for Ben to return. As he drove, Camacho asked Demarest what he thought Ben had done.

"I have no idea, and perhaps he did, in fact, get cold feet. That said, he's been very shrewd all along and it is highly possible he's got some scheme worked out. We really have no choice but to wait. I will call Sanders tomorrow and see if they have located our Mr. Clancy." The formerly cocky attorney was clearly unsettled.

That evening, over fresh local seafood, Agent Jackson finally got Ben to talk. His subject opened up to the federal employee about his youth and childhood and the incident that turned his life upside down. He explained that the perp was the new Pope and that the meeting in the attorney's office was to come to a settlement regarding the sexual assault he'd sustained, and that he was expected to take the money and remain silent.

"But you went right to the newspaper!" Jackson said, confused.

Ben nodded.

"I did what I felt was right," said Ben. "I didn't settle. Instead I took the papers – which I hadn't yet signed, you see?"

A look of understanding crossed Jackson's face.

"How much were they giving you?"

"Several million. That's not important though," Ben said. "I don't know that this will solve anything, but I had to try, I had to do something... right now. I may end up without a cent, but at least I'll have my dignity and know I didn't sell out."

"Phew," Jackson said. "You've got balls!"

Ben shrugged. "I was all set and ready to settle, walk away and be done with it, but then, after they tried to kill me ... Look, the money will never undo what's been done, right?" He explained. "In the end, they showed what utter pricks they are and that they clearly had no intention of making things right... No way now that I'll just accept it and walk away. There are thousands of others who've endured what I did at the hands of priests and others. Someone's got to call them out once and for all, and I figured that someone was me."

He yawned. The agent nodded.

"It's been a huge day," said Jackson. "And I'm sure you haven't slept well in weeks. I'm ready to call it a night, you?"

Ben nodded and bid goodnight to the agent. As they walked into their separate rooms, Ben called over his shoulder, "Can you do me a favor, though and fill Will Thomas in on the day's events? Tell him I'd like to talk to him first thing tomorrow morning if that's possible."

Jackson called Thomas and left him another voice mail. He then curled up in the living room with a good book after securing the premises. In a bedroom down the hall, Ben was already drifting off to sleep. Two additional federal agents kept watch from above and below the main house.

Ben awoke the next morning oddly refreshed after the excitement of the day before. After pouring a mug of coffee from the pot Jackson had kindly made, he grabbed *The New York Times* from the table where Jackson had already read it and glanced through it page by page. He hadn't expected the article to run and he was right. Still, there was another article bylined by Bradley about suspected Vatican ties to money laundering and he shook his head in wonder at the corruption of the esteemed organization.

Ben's cellphone rang as he was folding the paper.

"Hi, Will," Ben said realizing who it was. "Yeah, I was hoping things would break sooner so I could return home but not yet, I'm afraid," Ben said. "I do think things will happen that will take the pressure off me very soon, but I think until then, I better sit tight here if that works for you?"

He listened and then elaborated on the impending coverage in *The New York Times*.

"My thinking is, once it's out, they won't dare touch me," Ben said. "Would you agree?" Agent Jackson raised his eyes and listened as Ben continued to speak.

"Right, but in the end, I declined to settle. I realize that puts an even bigger bullseye on my head for the moment," Ben said, grinning, "But I have a lot of confidence in you guys."

His face grew serious now as he listened to the Senior Agent.

"Well, I may have gotten rich, but … This'll make it easier to live with myself in the long run," Ben said. "We can discuss it after it's all out there."

They talked a few minutes more and then Ben handed the phone over to his handler and went to pour himself another cup of coffee. He stepped out onto the deck and surveyed his surroundings. "I could be stuck in a worse place than this," he thought to himself. He took a moment to welcome the breeze from the Long Island Sound on his face and in his hair.

As expected, once Ben's assailant was identified, Thomas drove down to Brooklyn. Leaning on his network of sources, exercising warrants and backtracking telephone calls made recently, he traced the attempted hits on Ben's life to Madrone. Exerting pressure on the New York gangster in the form of the threatened arrest of his beloved grandson for trafficking in illegal drugs, Madrone, who had just been diagnosed with fourth stage liver cancer, confirmed his Italian connection.

"I may not be able to prove you set up the hit, but if one hair on my client's head is messed up," he said, leaning in toward Madrone. "I will come down here so fast, it will make your head spin, is that clear?"

"OK," the mobster shrugged.

"I didn't hear you," said Will Thomas, bearing down threateningly.

"I get it loud and clear," responded Madrone, sullenly.

Will left his place knowing he'd be back to arrest the crime boss once his case was further developed.

Thomas had Interpol pick up Vitale who had returned to his estate in Southern Italy. Based on intelligence gathered during their unobtrusive tail of the mobster identifying his recent meetings with Cardinal Bertolucci, Inspector Robert Giovanni, a 20 year veteran of the multi-national police force, spent several hours at the Vatican with two deputy inspectors grilling the Cardinal in the presence of several legal representatives for the Church. Bertolucci strenuously denied any knowledge of the "hit," but Giovanni was convinced that it was he who had in fact ordered it. It was just a matter of finding leverage on Vitale and Giovanni was confident he would find some.

Awakening to the smell of fresh coffee and a cool ocean breeze stirring the curtains, Ben strode to the kitchen, took up *The New York Times* which was handed him by Jackson and met Jackson's gaze. The agent's eyes told him this was the moment he'd been waiting for. Opening the folded paper, the headlines stared at Ben in the face.

"POPE ALLEGED PEDOPHILE!" Underneath the caption in dark letters the sub header read: "Vatican agrees to out of court settlement alleging Pope was pedophile while Headmaster at Elite NY Prep School."

Ben sank into the chair, engrossed in the multi-part article that portrayed the rape and sexual trauma Ben and the others had undergone, and detailed the ensuing traumas to their lives, even reporting on the resulting alcohol and drug abuse, mental illness, hospitalizations and PTSD. It did not mention the attempts on Ben's life but did disclose the terms of the rejected settlement. The remainder of the lengthy news passage named other victims of the Pope, and noted that other agencies such as the FBI and Interpol had been alerted and were cooperating in the ongoing investigation. The article was very clear and careful to note that while the other victims had signed confidentiality clauses, none who settled had broken their agreements. The *Times* had simply gotten the information in other ways and confirmed it through its own sources.

A second, breakout section of the enterprise piece probed the current political status of the Vatican, explored the possibility of UN sanctions against the Church and quoted RAVOC's leaders Brenda Lawson and Dan Callahan and others calling for the Vatican to make reparations to victims worldwide. This section also delved into the origins of the Vatican's sovereignty, noting that it had been granted that privilege by dictator Benito Mussolini during his Fascist reign of Italy. Further to the point, it cited calls by RAVOC and many other non-governmental victims' rights organizations to end Vatican City's diplomatic immunity. The article detailed several recent unsuccessful U.N. attempts to investigate the books of the Vatican Bank and quoted Brenda and others calling for public scrutiny of the Church's finances.

A third and final section of the coverage was a small info graphic. The chart showed the numbers of alleged victims raped or abused by members of the Catholic clergy on various continents around the world. The numbers were startling and dire.

Ben read the coverage twice and called Hugh Bradley at the *Times* to thank him. In turn, his cellphone was ringing constantly, and messages of congratulations and support were coming in fast and furious. Ben was relieved and felt a huge burden lifted off his shoulders. It was as if a large portion of his mission, his purpose in life, had been completely fulfilled. Could he go on now? Only time would tell.

News programs around the globe were all over the *Times* coverage, dissecting it and analyzing the allegations. One crafty reporter had honed in on Ben's residence only to find himself physically barred from entering. Another managed to find a former employer who spoke well of Ben but refused to speculate if the allegations were true or not as he simply did not know. A third tapped into the legal databases and identified Jamie who fortunately was visiting Brad per Ben's suggestion. Cable News talking heads were atwitter, trying to game the outcome of this sensational, once in a millennium breaking news development as they called it. Would the Pope step down? Would the Church remain sovereign? Would it be forced to pay reparations? So many questions to speculate over, so much air time to fill.

But it wasn't just the news media discussing the story. Cafes and shops around the world were buzzing with the story. For many Catholics this was the absolute last straw. These would never return to the Church. For many others, there was confusion, bewilderment, disgust, and in rare instances, even attempts at rationalization, however futile that might be. The fact is, His Holiness was not who he said he was.

As Ben's name was pronounced in public over and over, he called his son to check on him.

"How're you doing there, Brad?" Ben asked.

"Ok, really, and mom's doing well, too. We've turned off the tube and radio and I guess it kinda helped," said Brad. "How about you? How're you holding up, and when are you returning home to Connecticut?"

"I think I'll be heading there later today," Ben told him. "Is your mom there? Can I talk to her?"

"Sure, hang on," Brad said.

Jamie came to the phone and she and Ben spoke briefly. It was awkward to discuss something as earth-shattering and life-changing as had just taken place over the phone and they both knew it.

"I'll see you in a day or two, okay?" Ben asked as they said goodbye.

"Yes, of course!" Jamie answered. She was about to hang up, but spoke again. "Ben?"

"Yes, Jamie?" he said.

"I'm really proud of you," she said. "I now know what you've been going through all these years, and I'm, well..."

At a loss for words, she hesitated.

Ben felt a lump growing in his throat. "Jamie, thanks for that. We'll talk more in a day or so, okay? I really want to."

"I'd like that too, Ben" she replied.

After disconnecting, Ben called several others he trusted including Kelly, Brenda and Beth, all of whom were ecstatic at the developments. Then he dialed Carl.

"I see you've been quite busy these days," Carl said, pride ringing in his voice. "Bro, I'm, I really don't know what to say except I'm proud of you. You must've been going through hell. Way to navigate it, though."

"Thanks," Ben replied. "I have Paul to thank you know. He was a tremendous help, Carl. I owe him big-time."

"I'm not surprised," Carl said. "So, let's reschedule your visit in the next few days after things settle down a bit, huh?"

"Absolutely," Ben replied. "I have a lot to tell you!"

Ben disconnected from Carl as the telephone rang again. It was Will Thomas who was clearly pleased. "How the hell did you pull that off?" he asked Ben. Ben filled him in on the details and asked Will if he thought it was OK for him to go home. Will said he was quite confident that the mobster behind the two attempts wouldn't bother with Ben from here on in. It would be like closing the barn door after the horse ran out and surely, even these numb nuts would be savvy enough to realize that the links had all been identified, he told Ben.

"Right now, I kinda feel like I don't have a home after all the shit that went down there, you know?" Ben told him, "But I'm willing to give it a shot."

Will gave Jackson the go ahead to escort Ben back to Connecticut which he did as soon as Ben finished packing.

The two packed up the big sedan and drove northwest, taking the leisurely and pleasant ferry ride from Port Jefferson to Bridgeport, Connecticut. On the two hour journey, they relaxed and sat on deck, enjoying the fresh air. Thankfully, no one on the ferry recognized Ben.

Chapter 22
Certain Turmoil

After the *Times* articles hit the wires, all hell broke loose at the Vatican. Cardinals, priests and bishops scurried everywhere, ostensibly with important things to do, but in reality to find safety in the hopes things would blow over or at the very least, show the Pope's acts were those of a depraved man, isolated from the rest of the Church. It didn't help matters that so many of Alexander's efforts when he was head of CDF were now brought to the world's attention and scrutinized by journalists and policymakers everywhere in light of these new allegations. Tones were hushed, and ominous whispers abounded. It was as if the earth had fallen out from under the security of this once most holy and esteemed global monolith of piety.

In New York City, Brenda, Dan and others seized the momentum and worked night and day with delegates from the U.N. to lay out the framework for an international judicial body that would have enough teeth to hold the Pope and the Vatican accountable for their monstrous crimes. The *New York Times* series empowered and motivated those victimized by the Vatican and the myriad of organizations that worked on their behalf. Previously, these victims (and organizations) found themselves in an uneven battle against the Vatican's hegemonic resources, but now, in light of these new revelations, they had wind in their sails and an influx of massive public support to spread the word, and expand their resources. They also gained newfound support from global law enforcement officials and justice bureaus willing and ready to go after the criminals within the Church's hierarchy.

As Jackson drove north on Route 8, Ben watched the beautiful and lush summertime Central Connecticut scenery roll by. His apartment was cleaned and repaired the day before by a crime scene cleanup crew, courtesy of Agent Thomas and RAVOC's Connecticut team. As he entered his home, Ben shivered, recalling the shooting that had taken place only a few days ago, before consoling himself in the realization that it was all part of a bigger picture which was playing out right now here and across the world. Jackson waited outside in the hallway until Ben invited him in. Ben was to have a security detail for the next several days, until Thomas was convinced the threat had been removed.

At *The New York Times*, Hugh Bradley was busy working the phones, touching base with all contacts he could think of that might have information on the Pope. He knew there was even more to this story than had already been written. Though he had known about RAVOC from his previous work, including how the organization was founded and some of its major victories, the seasoned journalist was preparing a story on the organization for the following day. Thanks to the wire services, Bradley's enterprise piece the day before was picked up worldwide and was all over the internet as well. Bradley's email inbox was flooded with notes of approval, along with tips and allegations to follow on other clergy abuse incidents. There were a few pieces of hate mail, too, clearly written by church faithful who would never acknowledge or accept the reality of the criminal behavior exhibited by the Pope and others within the Church.

In Connecticut, Ben was on the phone with Kelly whose voice was brimming over with excitement over the several offers they'd received on the manuscript. There was a bidding war going on, she told him, and he smiled broadly. Even though he would never see a penny from the $25,000,000 settlement offered by the Vatican and St. Adolphus, he could still achieve some financial security for himself and his family after all. More importantly, he was navigating his way to the other side of this decades-long nightmare toward prosperity and wellness while maintaining his integrity.

Ben returned several other phone calls, the majority of which were related to his case and situation, including a conversation with Attorney Sanders.

"I hope you'll understand I did what I thought was necessary," Ben said. "I really appreciate all your efforts and will do my best to pay for the legal expenses you've accrued in handling my case."

"That would be appreciated, Ben, but I want you to know, you managed to resolve this better than any of us legal minds were able to. I'm very impressed with how you handled yourself and suspect in the end, you'll manage to recoup your settlement losses and then some."

"Well, thanks, sir. That means a lot to me and as a matter of fact, my sister's in discussion with some publishers right now…"

"Great, well, let me know if you need an attorney to look after your interests there. It's not my field but we have a couple of junior partners in the New York office that deal with publishing rights," Sanders said, and stopped for a moment before continuing. "In fact, give us that business and we'll forget about the expenses accrued thus far!"

"That sounds like a deal!" Ben said, all smiles now. Things were truly falling into place for him! He had one more call to make, and dialed Paul Adams, the man he literally owed his life to.

"If it weren't for your 'Plan B,' Paul, I think I would've caved..." Ben said sincerely. "I'm gonna find a way to make it up to you and I'd say we start by meeting up for a great steak dinner in the city. You name the place."

Paul laughed. "That sounds like a deal! I am glad things worked out so well, Ben".

In Vatican City, Cardinal Calderoni of Florence, and Cardinal Montagno from Genoa met over espresso at Montagno's offices at the Vatican. The two high-ranking prelates were plotting moves of their own, discussing what they felt was an unavoidable imperative. The pair, who had studied together at Seminary, were well-established in the College of Cardinals and were surprised when Mayron was elected Pope as they were on every Vatican-watchers' short list for that role for quite some time.

Younger, more naive men when John Paul I died just weeks after his election, the two Cardinals were unaware of the facts surrounding the incident that was kept out of the press due to the Vatican's rites of secrecy. A firm believer in transparency and diplomacy, John Paul was about to divulge secrets of the Vatican Bank and disclose the names of Catholic officials involved in freemasonry, a practice that was absolutely forbidden by the Church. The conspirators were many and numerous and most had ties to corrupt officials of the Italian Government and other organizations worldwide. To prevent this news from getting out, John Paul was poisoned, assassinated as he lay in the Papal bed. Though he had been in near perfect health, his reign lasted only a few short weeks, and the media and public had no idea he'd been murdered. Five years ago, when he discovered the truth of this, Montagno shared what he learned with Calderoni.

On this summer afternoon in a private courtyard over espressos, the two senior cardinals dismissed their aids and discussed the *New York Times* articles. After assessing the tremendous damage wrought the Vatican by the current Pope, and speculating over what might happen to the Church if things dragged on in an international court, they realized there was only one course of action they could take. Without much discussion, the two walked back to Montagno's apartment where he called the Vatican's chief physician, Cardinal Guillermo Lucchese, summoning him under the guise of an upset stomach. There, behind closed doors, the trio discussed the options that lay before them.

That same evening, heavy with shame and expecting the worst, Pope Alexander went to his quarters alone after dismissing his entourage. His physician was the last to check in on him around 10 p.m., a report by Italian authorities later concluded. Lucchese was the last person to see the Pope alive and when authorities interviewed him, he hinted at finding the Pope in a highly depressed and possibly suicidal mental state but one that the Pope denied and refused treatment for. Without Alexander's cooperation, Lucchese had no choice but to leave the Pope untreated for the night.

In the morning, Sister Margot, one of Alexander's attending nuns, entered the dark quarters and went to the windows to pull open the heavy velvet curtains. She let out a scream before blessing herself as she gazed at the horrific grimace on the face of the dead Pope. His body cold, he had clearly been dead for hours. Lucchese was urgently summoned, interrupting his morning rounds of sick patients, and rushed in with Cardinal Montagno who happened to be passing by. Breaking protocol in such cases, and before the Pope's Secretary entered the chambers, the two quickly called for a stretcher and ordered everyone else out of the room.

The physician closed the dead Pope's eyes which were open in a grotesque stare, and then his gaping mouth. They covered the body, and with a pair of attendants waiting outside, escorted it down to the morgue several floors beneath the city. Dismissing the attendants, as Montagno watched with fascination, Lucchese rapidly inserted a pair of tubes into the stiffening corpse, the first one, to drain the Pope's blood. The other, filled with formaldehyde to cover evidence of the poison administered the night before, was a glaring breach of Canon Law.

Later that day, authorities questioned both the physician and Cardinal Montagno, along with the Pope's attendants and others. An autopsy was ordered by Inspector Reynard of the Polizia de Stato, a move that was blocked by the Vatican's Secretary of State. "An autopsy is not allowed on His Holiness," the official told Reynard. "No Pope has ever undergone an autopsy, and none ever shall." Reynard included the quotes in his official report.

The papers the next day attributed the Pope's death to a heart attack due to large amounts of stress, but more than a few reporters smelled blood and found sources that alluded to either suicide or murder. Either way, even ordinary people viewed Alexander's timely death as a cover up and suspected that something else dark and nefarious issued from Vatican City.

The papers, cable news, blogosphere, and other media outlets hounded sources within the Vatican and the Italian State. They found several analysts now willing to discuss the Vatican's dark secrets from its foundation to the present day, but none that were solid sources able to confirm either murder or suicide in Alexander's case. In stories reporting the Pope's death they included Ben's case as the subheading coverage produced by most news agencies imaginable. The *Times* even offered a .pdf version of the entire settlement document on its website with a link to the *YouTube* uploaded audio of Attorney Demarest making the Church's pre-settlement apology statement. Coupled with the murder/suicide, there was little other news of interest for the entire next week. The shares of corporations with strong links to the Vatican fell precipitously, and the Euro even declined against the dollar, yen, and yuan when analysts predicted diminishing tourism in Rome.

Ben, still under guard, had foreseen most of this. Will Thomas, whom he now spoke with regularly, filled him in on a lot of the facts surrounding the investigation into the corruption in Vatican City and at the Vatican Bank. Will made it clear to Ben that by exposing so much of the Church's transgressions, Ben's actions had given the joint task force real teeth to delve deeper into the crimes and misdeeds carried out by the Church. They shared the belief that the Church had been in bed with "the devil" for a long time, and were glad the investigation had new life. Thomas assured Ben that his agency, Interpol, and Italy's own Guardia di Finanza were taking action and doing far more than just documenting these crimes.

Ben was keenly aware of keeping all his supporters closely informed. Since all the news broke, his Blog "The Daily Conspirator" was getting close to a million hits a day. Advertisers were throwing themselves at him and he knew he needed to delegate this to someone savvy enough to protect his interests. He approached Paul Adams

"I know you're retired, but I'm wondering if you'd like a little something to keep you out of trouble…" Ben said. "Would you sign on as my partner here?"

"Tempting, Ben!" Paul said. "Lets meet up and discuss it, shall we?"

Ben smiled, knowing he had an ally for life – and a savvy business partner he could count on as well.

The end game now lay in sight and after disconnecting with Paul, Ben called Brenda Lawson. She expressed genuine concern for Ben's safety, recognizing the Pandora's Box he had opened, but Ben reassured her that he was fine, and that he would be okay from here on in.

"And I think it's time, Brenda," he said matter of factly.

"Excuse me, what?" she asked.

"Well, you asked me a while ago to serve as RAVOC's representative to the U.N. It's time. I'm more than ready to take that responsibility on now, Brenda. And honored, too, if you'll still have me." Ben hadn't come this far to give up now.

"I'm so glad to hear that, Ben," Brenda responded, breathlessly. "You'll be perfect!" She didn't mention to Ben but she was already calculating the kind of reach and goodwill his name attached to RAVOC would generate. Goodwill and fundraising strength. A survivor in more ways than one, Brenda realized Ben's situation was going to place RAVOC on the global map. And she said as much to Ben.

"I'll be honest, Ben. It may sound cynical, but having your 'starpower' linked with RAVOC will do our organization a world of good," she admitted.

"Well, RAVOC helped me not only survive but also get past what I experienced as a kid, Brenda, and I owe the organization, quite literally, my life," Ben replied. "It's just that simple, and whatever I can do…"

The pair agreed to one other thing and two days later, with the Pope's story still hot on the press and in the people's minds, Brenda and Dan flew to New York City. Brenda used RAVOC funding to put Ben up in a decent midtown hotel and in his room, after dinner, Brenda, Dan, and Ben discussed the agenda for the following day. When they concluded the meeting around midnight, they all felt confident about how things would play out.

In Vatican City, there was utter shock and dismay. Not a single Cardinal wished for the position of Pope even though that position was now open. They were all afraid of stepping into the landmine there, distraught over the defensive position the church now found itself in. Not even the allure of control of the Vatican Bank's riches convinced any to exercise their ambition and put their name forward. Most felt they could get away with being a Cardinal and ride things out. The pandemonium continued, when, after two days not a single member of the College of Cardinals had enough tallied votes to become the next Vicar of St. Peter's.

In contrast to previous times, when black smoke was released from the Sistine Chapel, the Square outside St. Peter's was half empty, and a portion of those that were present were members of the press. At Mass the following Sunday, savvy reporters covering the Vatican noted that worldwide attendance was down markedly, as members of the faithful took their hearts, minds, and wallets elsewhere. It was as if a spigot had been closed, shutting down the Vatican's defining role in the course of human affairs. The victims in the sting were the Catholic faithful and they were at last catching on. The well-meaning foundations of the Church began its crumbling long ago, right into the hands of those whose greed and desire for power far outweighed the good intentions that lay in the Church's founders' and faithful followers' hearts.

Chapter 23
A World Transformed

Ben was exhausted from the ordeals of the last few weeks and spent as much quality time with Jamie and Brad as he could. After a short respite, with his own personal struggle nearly behind him, he stepped even further into the advocacy role, as promised, and made numerous calls to his friends – within RAVOC and other groups of similar interests around the globe, encouraging them to join him in asserting the necessity to create some body to try the Vatican on charges of Crimes against Humanity. He was astounded and greatly dismayed by the impotence of the U.N., even though he once believed in and admired the organization's ideals.

RAVOC and other international organizations contacted heads of state throughout the world, lobbying for justice and official scrutiny into the Vatican's wrongdoings. They reached out to representatives of each country to see if they could gain compliance for an oversight body, perhaps administered by

The Hague, to try the Vatican for its crimes. Some elected officials were reluctant to cooperate or put themselves on the line and it confirmed what they already knew: the Vatican's reach was indeed still very strong and powerful. Nonetheless, they were able to make some headway in gaining support.

Their break came when U.N. officials in the UK, Sweden, Norway, Germany, Ireland, Italy, and Canada agreed to sponsor a resolution calling for an evidentiary hearing at the International Court of Justice in Geneva, Switzerland. With support from enough other countries to pass the resolution, the Vatican would now finally be put on trial! The actual resolution called for an advisory proceeding review of the charges against those clerics found guilty of perpetrating sexual assaults on unsuspecting and innocent children as well as on the actions of their superiors. The resolution also called for filing of a separate contentious case against the Vatican by the signatory U.N. states to settle legal claims for economic damages caused by the Vatican's cover up efforts which kept these clerics in office and created more victims.

Though not a member of the United Nations, the Vatican, under the name Holy See, is a party to the statute of the International Court of Justice and as such, its actions are subject to ICJ review and action. The court was to convene the following month in Geneva and was to focus on the protection of children throughout the world with regard to sexual predators. Ben would of course be there, along with Brenda, numerous other survivors, and members of other organizations – government and NGO alike – to witness this historic event.

Ben took a break from trip preparations and convinced Brad to take a day off his work to go kayaking with him. Brad had a newfound pride for Ben as he saw him undertake the courageous battle he had just fought. He appreciated his father for sticking to his guns and keeping his integrity and principles intact.

The pair drove up to the Farmington River depot in Collinsville, where they rented a couple of kayaks. Ben capsized his getting in and had to get help getting the water out of it before they could go on their way. He was less used to this than Brad, a seasoned outdoorsman who did his share of whitewater kayaking. This was not whitewater, however, and was more relaxed and serene, the perfect setting to rekindle and reconnect. "Bucolic" was a word that came to Ben's mind. They paddled upstream for a solid hour or so, hung out for a while near the rapids which were just above them, then made their way back to the depot.

After returning the gear, the two men walked over to LaSalle's Market and Deli across the street for a late lunch. A young woman recognized Ben and placed a hand on his arm.

"Thank you so much for speaking out," she whispered. "My young son was abused and it has given me the courage to pursue matters more vigilantly." Unsure what to say, Ben simply patted her shoulder in consolation. She walked away silently as Ben and Brad stared after her.

After they ordered, and while waiting for their meal, they chatted easily. Brad asked Ben if this ordeal was now over for him.

"Not quite yet," Ben said. "There are still a few things left to do. In a way, it's never going to be over... There'll always be more battles to fight, but I feel like it is all forward progress from here."

Ben went into detail about the upcoming hearings at The Hague and what he hoped the ICJ could and would do.

"I have no clue what the end result will be but at least having a formal review will be a good, strong start. At the very least, the world will become fully aware of the Vatican's nefarious actions in covering up the clergy abuse. My dream would be for the court to call for an end to the Vatican's sovereignty but I'm not sure things would ever get that far.

Brad brought up Ben's public battle and, eyeing his father steadily, noted that it had taken tremendous courage and honesty to do what he'd done. Before they finished their meal, Brad looked closely at Ben and said seriously to his father: "I believe in you, Dad!"

"I believe in you, too," was Ben's short reply with a smile.

They drove home the rest of the way in good spirits, but in quiet, comfortably lost in their own thoughts. They parted for the evening and as Ben headed toward his own home after dropping Brad off, he took a longer route than necessary. His mind meandered back to his own parents. He couldn't blame them for what happened to him, after all, they did what they thought was right; they simply had no idea that such an evil act could have been perpetrated on one of their own children... and by a priest, no less. Still, he couldn't help but wonder what they would have thought about all this.

The following night he had Jamie over for dinner. He found her quiet, somewhat subdued and he tried to cajole her out of this somber place. She was a beautiful soul and he loved her deeply, but he had kept her at a distance for the last several months while he was going through this tremendous transition of his. He thought that it was time now to fill her in on all that had happened over the last few weeks, some of which she already knew.

"You sure do have a powerful story here. I'm glad you're OK." She said after he laid it all out for her.

They ate quietly, but locking eyes over the table often and smiling, as if to reassure each other of the peace between them, and then Ben drove her home. As he drove, though, he told her of the advance the publishing company had given him and that he would be moving soon. He still had hopes that the two of them could one day really count on each other's love and affection, and make a fresh start of it. He let Jamie know all this.

"We'll see," she said simply.

Ben came home to his small apartment and, on powering up the computer, perused some real estate websites in northern New England. He was seeking a ranch house with at least 5 or 6 acres of land, and he knew he could find something suitable. This would offer him the fresh start he sought after this long, painful journey.

He called Attorney Sanders the following day.

"Where have you been?" The attorney inquired emphatically. "We still may have a settlement with the Jesuits, despite the fact that the Pope has now died, and even though you blew the cover off this whole thing! Will you agree to a settlement now?"

"Sure," Ben said.

"Good, I'll discuss this with Camacho and see what they're willing to offer... On another subject, I assume you will be going to Geneva?" the attorney asked.

"Absolutely!" said Ben, "How about you?"

"Oh, I'll be there alright" the attorney said with a lighthearted yet determined tone. "My partner's agreed to take on my caseload so I can be part of this."

Later that evening, Kelly called Ben After he updated her on all he had been through, she stopped him. Her voice shook a little when she went on.

"You know, Ben, your courage and tenacity has changed things not only for you, but for many others," she said. He couldn't see it but she was wiping at her eyes as she went on. "You've given a voice to so many by your actions, even me!"

"Oh, thanks, Kel, your words mean so much to me, ya know?" Ben said and then changed the subject abruptly.

It was obviously coming together for Ben. After years of living on the edge and sometimes even in the shadows, it was all gelling. Everything he believed in before he lost his innocence was beginning to come true. He had learned many years ago that he could live like a king on very little, as long as he kept his honesty and his integrity intact. But now, his time would be his own, no more working menial jobs to make ends meet and survive. He now had the freedom to choose where and how to live, and most importantly, the opportunity to continue to make this world a better place for himself and those he loved.

Attorney Sanders followed up with him the next day to advise him that the original offer had been retracted, given his failure to comply with the confidentiality clause, but the Jesuits were now offering, for full restitution of damages, a sum of $500,000. It was not much in comparison to the initial amount, but with this, Ben had ultimately gotten what he wanted after all. Full accountability *and* disclosure of the Pope's and the Church's misdeeds, as well as a modest financial sum as compensation for his suffering and losses. While it certainly didn't come close to what a seasoned actuary would have calculated for his losses and suffering endured, he was pleased with it all the same. Besides, he now had an international platform to work with, including a significant advance on a potential bestselling memoir.

Chapter 24
International Scrutiny

Practically overnight, RAVOC became the go-to organization recognized worldwide in its fight for children's rights and for justice for survivors of clergy sexual assault. Following *The New York Time's* expose, the organization was gaining in prominence in Ireland, Germany, Belgium and the rest of Europe.

Times reporter Hugh Bradley covered the lobbying efforts of RAVOC and other like-minded organizations at the UN and met and talked with Ben on his first high-profile visit to the U.N. Ben in turn introduced Bradley to RAVOC's founders Brenda Lawson and Dan Callahan who the reporter previously interviewed via telephone but had never met in person. Bradley was attentive and sharp, fully aware that history was being made. He planned to report on the implications of what was taking place and its impact on the entire world, not just on the Catholic Church in the U.S. He questioned RAVOC's founders with insight regarding the desired and anticipated outcome of their efforts and the upcoming ICJ hearings. He also asked their opinion on several new clergy abuse cases he had recently received tips on. Although as a reporter, he had to maintain impartiality, it was clear they had gained a strong ally in the fight against clergy abuse, and they knew any coverage he could provide would benefit RAVOC and the cause.

Three weeks later, when he changed planes at Chicago's O'Hare Airport, Ben met up with Brenda Lawson for the eight-hour flight to Geneva where they sat together in a pair of comfortable seats in business class. Before settling in for some sleep, they familiarized themselves with the emissaries attending the hearings. Ben commented enthusiastically on the number of representatives from the various countries and organizations involved, as the list was quite extensive. Brenda cautioned Ben that they still had an uphill battle on their hands, but both agreed they did not come this far to give up now.

Landing at Geneva International Airport early the following morning, Ben and Brenda were lucky and breezed through customs, immigration and got a cab right away. Once checked in and situated in their rooms across the hall from one another, each took a short catnap. At eight p.m., refreshed and hungry, they met at the elevators, went down and gathered in the hotel's expansive lobby with a number of fellow advocates who had arranged to meet there. The large group – perhaps 30 in all, dined in the Michelin-rated hotel restaurant, spotting several officials who would be involved in the upcoming hearings in conversation just a few tables away. Though some were tempted, none from their party approached the delegates, not wanting to disturb them in any way.

The trial was scheduled to start the next morning at the Peace Palace in The Hague under tight security. While Ben and the other advocates were preparing for this all-important hearing, for the second time in a month the Conclave for the College of Cardinals could not decide on the next Pontiff.

"Fumata Nera! Black Smoke from the Sistine Chapel!" the headlines read the following day. St. Peter's Square was half empty in the late summer morning, in stark contrast to previous papal elections. So, too, was attendance at mass the following Sunday throughout the entire world.

Though he was tired, before turning in that evening Ben called Jamie through his Skype account. He was brimming over with enthusiasm and told her about his impressions of people he'd regarded as important to the movement but that he'd never met before, including Brenda.

"I'm so glad it is going well, Ben." Jamie responded. "I am really proud of how you have followed through on this."

"Thanks, that means so much to hear you say that. You know I love you Jamie!" Ben said almost breathlessly.

"I love you, too, Ben, please be safe!" she answered, somewhat noncommittally. They talked a bit longer and then disconnected, after which Ben called Will Thomas, the agent who had protected him several weeks earlier. He updated Will on the activities in Geneva and the pair traded insights and speculated on the court proceedings. A true professional, Will was always careful not to overstep his bounds. However, he did mention that the investigation into the attempts on Ben's life was working with assets from the FBI and Interpol and he felt confident those who ordered the hits were in Italy. Ben understood what he meant, but left it at that for now to focus solely on the hearings of the commission.

He had tried before he left and missed him, so before he turned in, Ben had one more call to make. Paul Adams answered the phone with curiosity, not sure who the mystery number belonged to.

"Oh, hey, Ben! How's it going over there?" he asked. "It looks like a really important time for you!"

"Definitely, Paul," Ben said. "And thanks to you, man! Seriously, I cannot thank you enough and want to know what I can bring back for you?"

Paul laughed and thought for a moment. "Nothing, really, just get the job done, you got it?"

"Absolutely. Keep watching the news!" Ben replied. "Well listen, I better go now, it's getting late here. Take care and thanks again for everything, Paul."

After disconnecting the call, Ben set his IPhone to charge and lay his head on the pillow, exhausted from the transatlantic flight and time change, despite the two-hour nap earlier in the day. It took only a few minutes for him to fall asleep. The next morning he awoke refreshed and joined Brenda for a light breakfast after which the two boarded a shuttle for the trip to the Peace Palace. As they entered, to Ben it seemed the air was electrically charged, the anticipation surrounding the court hearings was tremendous.

When the session opened, the Chief Prosecutor of the judicial proceedings, Prime Minister of Norway, Oleg Gustafson, read a statement into the record that provided a framework around which the court would work and set the tone for the proceedings.

"To abuse the rights and the very lives of children is to abuse the rights of all in our world. No longer will we, as a world community tolerate these crimes, for crimes they are and heinous ones at that, no matter what cloak they are hidden under. We must turn the page for a new humanity, a bold New World that embraces the dignity of each individual.

In holding these proceedings, we are establishing the precedent for just such a mindset."

"We have created an unsafe society where force and abuse are commonplace. The number of the victims is so huge as to be staggering and beyond imagination or comprehension. Ladies and Gentlemen of the court, this gathering here is historic in every way. You hold the keys to the kind of world where our youths can live and grow without fear. None of us are naive enough to think that we can solve all the ills of our times, but we can make significant progress by shedding a light most keenly on those who would rape, molest, or in any other way, abuse the innocent in the guise of spiritual leader or other authority figure."

Gustafson was interrupted by thunderous applause from the audience as the Chief Justice pounded a gavel. Gustafson then held up a hand to the crowd and continued.

"An acceptable norm, the only acceptable norm in this regard is zero tolerance. In this court, we say 'No More!' We call for an ethical revolution starting here and now that addresses the well-being of every youngster on this planet whether from Africa or Asia or the United States; from Germany or Italy to Mexico, Ecuador, Brazil, Greece, etc. We ask you to draw a line and say "never again will we allow this type of behavior on the face of the earth."

The Vatican's defense team spoke next, addressing the court and ignoring those in the public gallery who were fidgeting and talking under their breath. At the end of the first day, a very clear position had been laid out. Over the next several days, the Justices would have an opportunity to question the legal teams from both sides and hear from specially designated individuals.

In Rome, in St. Peter's Square, for the third time in as many weeks, black smoke poured from the windows of the Sistine chapel. Many suspected that something was going dreadfully wrong inside. When he learned of the failure to name a successor, Ben imagined chaos and confusion, where fear and uncertainty reigned. He was right. No more was this the bastion of Christianity, but only a pitiful gathering of old men lacking a vision about the future of their institution. As he read further in the international news, he noted that there were fewer and fewer people milling about St. Peter's Square each day.

Ben was called to speak as a victim and survivor during the second week of the hearings. Telling his story, Ben recalled in narrative form all he had endured, choking back tears at several different points in front of these thousands of witnesses. He did not read from a prepared statement or script, but instead spoke from the heart and presented several facts not yet introduced into evidence about sexual assault and molestation of children at the hands of clergy and other religious leaders.

After his testimony, during which the entire arena was silent, Brenda was called up to testify as RAVOC's leader. She presented a number of statistics about sexual trauma and abuse that had been obtained from the Australian think-tank The World Alliance. Most present in the gallery were aware of the numbers but restating them was important for the judges and news outlets covering the events and Brenda distributed handouts including the statistics she had testified to for their later review.

At the end of the third full week of hearings, to celebrate the concluding testimony, Ben and Brenda joined several other members of their team at the Restaurant Les Amures at the Rue du Puits, with a four star international rating, offering delicious Austrian, German and Swiss fare. Though Brenda was highly budget-conscious, a benefactor recently donated a magnanimous contribution to cover all of their expenses for the duration of the trip and two year's operating expenses for RAVOC as well.

The restaurant was set on a picturesque corner in Geneva's Old Town, and Ben waited just outside in the early September air while the rest of the party steadily arrived. They sat at a round table in the corner and ordered drinks from a friendly Swiss waitress.

Brenda watched Ben and noticed that he did not order anything alcoholic. She thought about him and beamed with pride at the challenges he had recently overcome to get to this place. This entire affair was molding him into a leading spokesperson on this subject and she was proud he was aligned with RAVOC. When the check came, Brenda picked up the tab for the entire table, overriding all arguments, explaining she would expense it back to RAVOC which silenced her fellow diners' protests. In exchange, though, she asked for all to pose for a group photo that she would include with a gracious note of appreciation to RAVOC's benefactor.

Again, for the eighth time in three weeks, thick black smoke was seen through the Sistine Chapel's high arched windows. Once more, very few were present in St. Peter's to witness the event. The media was covering this inability to name a successor almost as an afterthought, leading into the coverage by posing the question of whether the Vatican would ever recover from the damage Alexander and his predecessor, Pope Boniface, had wrought.

During an afternoon break that last day, the Chief Prosecutor, Prime Minister Gustafson phoned up several members of the Italian Parliament that he had met at a conference in Rome two years earlier. Having won their trust with his warmth and congeniality, he now needed a favor, a very big one. As he had been listening to all of the testimony these past weeks, he became deeply troubled and wanted the Italian lawmakers to take a good hard look at the Lateran Treaty of 1929 between Benito Mussolini and the Catholic Church. Resolving the "Roman Question" when in 1870 Rome was captured and became part of unified Italy, the 1929 treaty gave Vatican City not only great wealth, but international sovereignty as well.

Gustafson asked the Italian lawmakers if they might find a way to overturn it. He hinted that the ICJ's findings would most likely be against the Vatican and added that the Vatican had not complied with the U.N. to turn over promised documents regarding childhood sexual abuse by priests. The lawmakers could posit, he suggested, that the Vatican's disregard for U.N. requirements posed a danger for Italy's own standing within the U.N.

"I am not trying to tell you how to comport yourselves, and of course your country's internal interests are your own concern," he said, "but perhaps considering the added economic benefit of including the Church in your country's tax rolls would perhaps entice those reluctant to consider it for moral reasons."

Encouraged by their responses, he placed a call to the Prime Minister of Italy who assured him he was in favor of the move and would look into the matter with due haste. After disconnecting with his colleague, Gustafson felt that they were indeed on the brink of re-writing history. He returned to the courtroom feeling like the proceedings had accomplished a significant amount.

When the decision was announced, a clear majority of judges found against the Vatican and bad actors within the Church. Severe and just restitution was to be made by the Vatican in varying amounts to each country whose citizens had been documented victims of clergy abuse. The judgment, totaling 430 billion Euros, was to be divided up based on a formula the court's actuaries had developed. Other sanctions would be established, but individually with each victimized country's delegation.

Chapter 25
Closure

Ben and Brenda were ecstatic and like everyone else in the Peace Palace, unselfconsciously displayed their relief and joy, hugging neighbors, strangers, and even shedding tears. The tide had finally turned, and now people everywhere could expect more security for their children in religious and educational environments. For one brief instant, Ben's thoughts flashed back to the ghost of that young school boy he had once been years before, filled with shame as he scurried through the hallways to exit that evil place. His mind didn't linger there long, however, as their group was having a celebratory dinner that evening.

They had agreed on an Indian restaurant only a few blocks away. Ben had never tried Indian food before but was game. As he looked around the expansive table, he realized this was an experience Jamie would have enjoyed. He found a wireless connection and Skyped her. It was midday in New England,

and unfortunately, she was working so he left her a message, sharing with her the great news that the hearings were over and that he'd be home the next night. He walked back into the restaurant and surveyed his fellow advocates. From all different origins, they all had one thing in common and he was very proud to share that passion for justice with them.

The next day as he and Brenda walked quickly through Geneva's international terminal readying for their flight home, Ben saw that the news had reached home. "Victory for human rights!!!" cried the *New York Times* headline. "Victims 1, Vatican 0" *Le Monde* shouted. Nearly every major paper in the world had above-the-fold front page coverage of the court's decision. Ben and Brenda walked through the security lines with several new friends they made while at the hearings and said farewell in the concourse before making their way to Gate 34 to board their flight back to the States.

Once in the air, Ben and Brenda made small talk before catching some sleep. Though they were going to have an easier adjustment to the time difference flying back to the states, they had stayed up very late the night before celebrating with their colleagues and both were exhausted. As Ben slept on that transatlantic flight, a great deal of news was breaking in Italy. The occupants of Row B-4 did not realize it, but their final hope was becoming a reality.

At the Vatican, for the ninth time in three weeks, the chimney from the Sistine Chapel spewed black smoke, and once more, as it wafted into the air, only a few bystanders observed this occurrence. Inside, no one stepped forward to become Pontiff, even with the lure of control of the Vatican Bank, although its balances were dwindling rapidly. Worse, no one Cardinal was thought to have the leadership material to guide the Church through these rocky times.

In Rome, at the seat of Parliament that same day, an Italian member of the Senate introduced a bill overturning the 1929 Lateran Treaty made between Benito Mussolini and the Vatican. A year earlier, the esteemed lawmaker would have expected outrage, perhaps even calls for his ouster. This time, however, there was productive and efficient dialogue as lawmakers put aside ideology for the sake of country and common sense. It became an easy decision once they reviewed the revenue side of the measure as well as the ethical one. Parliament swiftly passed the bill, and by 9 p.m. that same day, the Prime Minister signed it into law.

The public explanation was Italy's need for greater revenue on the home front. After all, the Catholic Church was the largest landowner in Italy, as it was in the rest of the world. Vatican City had just lost its sovereignty and would now be forced to pay taxes – albeit marginal ones assessed all religious entities -- on all its holdings. As importantly, the Roman Catholic Church would be subject to the same scrutiny that any ordinary secular organization would have to endure. Representatives of the Vatican publicly protested the measure, but as it was in such disarray, without an official leader, the cries fell on deaf ears.

Ben woke up on approach to O'Hare International Airport where the local time was 5:15 p.m. Powering on their cellphones after wheels down, both he and Brenda flashed anxious looks at one another noting they each had multiple voice mails from various people close to them.

"Oh my gosh! I hope nothing's wrong," Brenda said as she started to listen. Within moments, the full realization of what had happened in Italy sunk in and the two hugged one another, still seated, as the A-300 taxied to the gate. Both Brenda and Ben wiped away tears, realizing the enormity of what had just happened. Around them, other passengers were watching with curiosity. Brenda smiled and shared with a mostly confused audience the historic news.

"They wouldn't understand," Ben thought to himself as he saw their blank faces.

After landing and clearing customs and immigration, the ecstatic pair hugged one another, said brief goodbyes, and went their separate ways. Ben found his gate and read the updates about Italy's move on his IPhone and let his mind wander as he sipped coffee on the commuter flight to New York. He thought about the millions and millions of formerly devout Catholics, likely now shaken to their cores. He hoped that, just as he had experienced for himself, worlds of new opportunities and new hope would open up to them, these millions of good, decent people. He hoped this major turn of events would have a tremendous positive impact on the future for all humankind. Perhaps it would herald in a new dawn, an age of reason and enlightenment.

Landing in Hartford, he grabbed his bags, caught the airport shuttle service, and on the way back to his apartment, he called Jamie and asked if she wanted to go out for a bite.

When they met an hour later in Jamie's doorway, she hugged then kissed him and said: "I'm so proud of you! What are you going to do now that it's over?"

Ben replied with a loving smile: "Move to Vermont and take care of you."

They had dinner and went home together arm in arm.

In Vatican City, after nearly eight weeks of chaos and deliberation, a new Pontiff was finally chosen. To celebrate this election, white smoke emerged from the Sistine Chapel. St. Peter's Square was virtually empty except for the pigeons that gathered near the statues. The next day, on page 13 of a small Italian newspaper, the identity of the new Pope was revealed. A new day has indeed dawned!

Chapter 26
About Paul

Paul Adams never fully explained why he was so committed to Ben and this cause, but watched the proceedings in Geneva with great interest. And as he did, he couldn't help but think about his daughter. As the proceedings dragged on, Paul found himself spending more and more time in the room once occupied by his little girl.

Years before, while he was serving with the Diplomatic Corps in Japan, his bright and vivacious 15-year-old daughter, Vanessa, attended an all-girls preparatory school back in the states. She was filled with academic curiosity and promise, and was a singularly gifted athlete as well. Paul and his wife, Mary, had wrestled with the idea of allowing their little girl to remain stateside. After weighing all the options, they decided it would be best for her future, chose the perfect school and Vanessa was very happy there for several months.

After they learned of her molestation, Paul and Mary brought Vanessa to live with them in Tokyo, hoping to ease her burden and offer solace to her heart. They also thought the exciting cultural experience of life in Tokyo was unlike anything she'd ever had before and would help her in her transition. Unfortunately, Vanessa could never get past the rape and assault by her high school Soccer coach, despite extensive family and individual therapy sessions. She rarely smiled and had much difficulty in bonding with others. Her parents did what they could to aid in her recovery but she faced a constant daily battle in overcoming her very serious depression. As she became more familiar with her new surroundings, Vanessa sought solace in easily accessible drugs she obtained while out clubbing, something she hid from her parents. When the police came to the door early one morning, Paul and Mary fell into one another's arms and sank into a dark hole: their daughter had died on the way to the hospital of an overdose.

Seeking vengeance, answers, and solace in staying busy, Paul and Mary went through extensive counseling. Seeking further answers, Paul was directed to the World Alliance, a not-for profit organization for survivors of sexual trauma based in Australia. Particularly noted for its ability to gather and attach significance to statistics, Paul began to study their information and was stunned to discover that one of six men and fully 25 percent of all women worldwide are abuse victims. The organization conducted regression analysis and reported that the impact these crimes had in terms of a country's sociological and economic costs were staggering. He became obsessed with the issue and found himself falling further and further down a rabbit hole of darkness, isolating himself from Mary and his work.

Months after Vanessa's death, Mary returned stateside to live in their family brownstone in Brooklyn Heights, close to the cemetery where their only child was buried. Paul found in work and research a great escape and as months turned into years, the couple grew apart until one day, Mary left Paul for another man.

Now, years later, retired and living alone in a house filled with reminders, Paul was finally able to lay his daughter's memory to rest. In the dark, he raised his glass and drank a toast to Ben Clancy knowing that without his courageous stand, these atrocities would have continued without recourse. As he watched the sun rise, Paul realized it was indeed, a very new world.

About the Authors

E. Brian Walsh

A victim of clergy sex abuse himself, E. Brian Walsh is now a member of two international advocacy organizations addressing sexual abuse, Survivor's Network of those Abused by Priests (SNAP) and Australian-based The Global Alliance. Walsh is a self-published non-fiction writer and songwriter based in New England. Much like the protagonist, he was a rising star at Regis High School, the elite Jesuit prep school in New York City. He attended Notre Dame University and is now a student of eastern philosophy.

M.W. Satchell

A former journalist for *The Tennessean,* and published in *The New York Times, USA Today,* and internationally, Maura Satchell dabbles in writing and screenwriting. As Brian's sister, Maura also received a Catholic School education and witnessed firsthand the long-term consequences of her brother's experience as a clergy sex abuse victim.

More from Four Pillars Media Group
www.fourpillarsmediagroup.com

If you enjoyed **The Crumbling Empire**, watch for

The Song of Revolution,

Second book in the Ben Clancy series coming in 2014. Ben deserves a break after taking on the Vatican, but that is not in the cards. Instead, he gets drawn in to the global economic crisis and the political turmoil surrounding it.

Other books from FPMG you might also enjoy:

Spyder's Web

A lighthearted murder mystery in the Agatha Christie style by Ian Mayo-Smith.

Eavesdropping on Adolph Hitler

Ian Mayo-Smith's true account of his work in World War II as a code breaker at the world famous Bletchley Park cryptography center. Coming soon.

My Life with AIDS, Tragedy to Triumph

Catherine Wyatt Morley's account of her life as a faithful wife and mother of three children who was infected with the HIV AIDS virus by her unfaithful husband. Her journey, born out of tragedy, culminates in the triumphal *Self Magazine* 2012 Women Doing Good recognition of her efforts as an HIV/AIDS activist who named her a 2012 Women Doing Good honoree.

www.ingramcontent.com/pod-product-compliance
Lightning Source LLC
Chambersburg PA
CBHW072206170626

46813CB00003B/820